SAVING AIMEE

SAVING MARGO

BARBARA J. DESMAN

WHAT'S NEXT PUBLISHING

Saving Aimee/Saving Margo

Published by What's Next Publishing

Copyright © 2022 by Barbara Desman

ISBN (Print): 978-1-66783-5-716
ISBN (eBook): 978-1-66783-5-723

Dedication

This story is dedicated to all the

victims of human trafficking.

May we never stop saving them.

"There are risks and costs to action. But they are far less thàn the long range costs of comfortable inaction."

—JOHN F. KENNEDY

PREFACE

When I began to weave Margo's story of love, loss, guilt, and redemption, I had no idea she and I would encounter human trafficking.

In July of 2016, I attended a meeting at my church aimed at educating us about our new mission of focusing on the problem of human trafficking in our community. A detective from the Special Victims Unit of the Scottsdale Police Department, AZ, began by telling us we might think we knew who these victims were; that we probably thought they were all poor, drug addicts, runaways, and illegals, and while that was sometimes true, they could also be from affluent families right here in Scottsdale as was his first case. He went on to describe the tactics the traffickers use on these girls and while, in many cases, they are abducted, some are "groomed" by their captors. This is referred to as the Romeo or Loverboy technique whereby a vulnerable young person is lured with promises of love and affection and access to a glamourous lifestyle.

Our church decided to partner with The Phoenix Dream Center to support their mission to help the victims of human trafficking. Since opening in September of 2008, the human trafficking recovery program at the Phoenix Dream Center has served over 1200 girls and young women, mostly between the ages of 13 and 26 years old. The girls spoke to us about their experiences. I wanted to help them. It occurred to me that Margo's story could provide a way to bring awareness of this despicable enterprise to an audience who would not otherwise be drawn to the subject of human trafficking.

Prior to the passage in the United States of the Trafficking Victims Protection Act (TVPA) signed into law on October 16, 2000, the general public had little awareness of the subject of human trafficking and sex trafficking except to believe it was something that happened in other parts of the world. With the enactment of the TVPA, the United States took a lead in combating human trafficking, prosecuting traffickers, and protecting victims.

Because of this, I've chosen to set Margo's story in the '90s when the major center for human trafficking was Thailand and little was known about it in the United States. While this is not just a story about human trafficking, it's my hope that the reader will learn from the experiences of Aimee and Margo, and perhaps be moved, as I was, to become involved in raising awareness, and supporting places like the Phoenix Dream Center. For more information, go to their website: phoenixdreamcenter.org.

Now, let's meet Margo.

CHAPTER 1

MARGO

January 1998

At first, Margo wasn't sure it was really the ringing of her phone that woke her. She groaned and rolled over to check her alarm clock. She had only been in bed for a couple of hours. No one ever called her except her nephew Eric, and he knew not to disturb her before three in the afternoon.

She swung her legs over the side of the single bed and sat up. Sliding her hand across the nightstand, her fingers groped for the receiver as her eyes adjusted to the dark. She hoped they weren't calling her to come in to work early. It had been a very busy Saturday night. The news about an affair between President Clinton and an intern named Monica Lewinsky was all the other reservations agents could talk about. Margo stayed out of it. She understood about secrets.

"Is this Margo Kitteridge?"

"Who's calling?"

"This is Detective Sam Carpenter of the Los Angeles Police Department. Are you the mother of Aimee Gordon?"

Suddenly awake, Margo pulled herself off the bed and struggled to stand, her heart pounded in her ears as she clutched the receiver. *Aimee? She had only recently heard her name for the first time. She hadn't expected to hear it again so soon or in this way.*

"We understand that you are Aimee Gordon's birth mother, Mrs. Kitteridge. Is that true?"

Margo sucked in her breath. Her mouth went dry.

"Yeah, yes," she said, stammering, "but she was adopted out." *That sounded awful*, she thought and quickly added, "I've been trying to find her recently. Why are you calling me? How did you get my name?"

"Her adoptive parents provided us with your name. I'm calling to inform you that she's missing and may be in trouble. We'd appreciate it if you could come down to the station to answer a few questions."

"Trouble? What kind of trouble?" Margo tried to keep the panic out of her voice.

"I'd rather talk in person. When can you come down to the station? We're in downtown L.A. at 100 W. First Street."

She slumped back down on the edge of the bed and pushed the tangled hair off her face. Her mind was spinning.

"I work at night. I guess I can come when I get off tomorrow morning if that's all right. I can probably be there by nine."

"That will be fine. I'm on the second floor, room 224. Just ask for Detective Carpenter. Thank you, Mrs. Kitteridge."

"It's Miss Kitteridge," correcting him, as she hung up the phone. *Aimee in trouble? Why was she missing? Did they think she had anything to do with Aimee's disappearance?* She hadn't known where Aimee was for eighteen years, and now, she was missing. Margo's throat tightened and tears stung her eyes.

She knew she wouldn't be able to go back to sleep. She needed to call her best friend, really her only friend.

Margo and Kathy met as ticket agents at the Seattle airport. Margo's parents were not happy when Margo announced she was not going to college because she wanted to work for an airline.

"I've always wanted to travel. When Johnny graduates from college and we get married, we'll see the world together," Margo had told them.

Margo and Johnny were high school sweethearts. There was an understanding that they would marry when Johnny finished college. At least that was what Margo thought.

Her older sister Anne was already a sophomore. She had always been focused on how her life was going to go. She would meet her future husband in college, get married, and have kids. Those were the plans their parents had for both of them. So, when Margo told them she wasn't going to college, they did what they usually did with Margo, they shook their heads.

Margo and Kathy liked each other immediately and decided to room together. When Johnny broke up with her, it was Kathy who was there for Margo through the tears, the anger, the sadness, and the Rocky Road ice cream.

When Kathy joyfully announced her engagement, she took Margo's hands in hers and said, "Now that I'm getting married and moving out, I think you need to get out of Seattle. I heard there's an opening at the ticket counter in Los Angeles. Why don't you put in for a transfer? I'll miss you terribly, but I think it would be good for you."

That's what Margo did and they had remained friends all these years.

"Hi, Kath, is it too early to call?"

"No. What are you doing up? You sound upset."

"I just got a call from the LAPD! The detective asked me if I was Aimee Gordon's biological mother!"

"What?"

"They want me to come down to the station." She choked back the lump forming in her throat. "They say she's missing and may be in trouble."

"What kind of trouble?"

"I don't know. He wants me to come down there to talk about it."

"How did they know about you?"

"Her parents gave them my name. You know I just found out last week who adopted Aimee and where they live. I was so happy to even know a little about her and now she's missing."

"Did you try to contact her?"

"No, no."

"Well, just go down and see what it's all about. This is your chance to find out more about her and the people who adopted her. She would be eighteen, right? Maybe she ran away."

"I hope they don't think I might have something to do with her being missing. That maybe I know where she is."

"Well, you don't, so you have nothing to hide. When are you going to the station?"

"Tomorrow morning, after I get off work."

"Call me the minute you get home. Now, try to get some sleep."

"Thanks, Kath, I don't know what I'd do without you."

CHAPTER 2

Anyone passing Margo on the sidewalk would have made a wide arc away from her or may have even crossed to the other side of the street. You didn't have to be near her to sense she hadn't bathed in a while. Her brown hair hung in stringy strands down to shoulders that slumped from the weight of the plastic shopping bags she carried. The stained, green T-shirt hung down loosely over a long black skirt of indeterminate fabric. The leopard print bedroom slippers she wore made her shuffle like a woman much older than her age.

Her car sitting in the employee parking lot looked as unkempt as its owner. Its original black paint was peeling, and it bore many a ding. The back seat was filled with cardboard boxes, empty plastic water bottles, various bags, and food wrappers. The dashboard was piled high with wads of used tissues. But Margo didn't care. It got her where she needed to go, and she never worried about it being stolen.

Yes, you might have thought to call her a bag lady, a sight not uncommon in the seedy part of Los Angeles where she lived unnoticed.

But Margo wasn't homeless. She had a one-bedroom apartment in South Los Angeles, not far from the airport and her company's headquarters. It was furnished with the bare necessities—a tattered brown sofa and easy chair from Goodwill. A wooden table and four mismatched chairs separated the living room from the walk-up kitchenette. One window in the living room and one in the bedroom provided a dingy view of the apartment house next door and the alleyway between them. Margo had hung heavy gold and brown striped drapes that could be pulled together to keep the sun and the world out while she slept during the day. A small television sat atop a bookcase, its rabbit ear antenna scanning the air for the local channels. A single bed was covered with blue sheets and a yellow cotton blanket. Next to it, a flea-market wicker nightstand supported a goose-necked lamp and a stack of books.

In stark contrast to the dreary setting was the rainbow of color provided by designer dresses, suits, blouses, and sweaters that hung on a metal clothes rack along one wall of the bedroom. The closet was filled with stacks of shoeboxes housing pumps, wedges, and boots with names like Jimmy Choo and handbags from Kate Spade. These did not belong to Margo; it all belonged to Margurite.

Rumors about Margo were rampant in the company; even employees who worked days and in other departments knew about this eccentric woman. She had attained the status of an urban legend. Fueling the rumors was what they called, "Margo's vacation transformation". When she came to work on her last night shift before she embarked on vacation, she was almost unrecognizable. Her chestnut-colored hair was no longer unkempt. It was shiny and fell in soft curls that framed her oval face. Her naturally long eyelashes were darkened by mascara. Her soft brown eyes no longer looked dead. The sloppy, stained T-shirt and long black skirt were replaced by a Diane Von Furstenberg floral print wrap dress that showed off her slim, curvy figure and perfectly shaped calves. Wedge heels replaced the bedroom slippers revealing manicured toes.

The first time this happened, her co-workers were astonished to see this pretty, stylish woman who had just been discovered the night before spending her break curled up in a grimy gray sleeping bag in the telephone equipment room. They didn't like the fact that they had to work next to the "bag lady" Margo but because they were working in a windowless reservations office at night with no face-to-face contact with the customers, there was no dress code. Margo had been with the company for over twenty years and was an expert in handling difficult customers so management turned a blind eye to her idiosyncrasies. She kept to herself. She was a hard worker and took any holiday and overtime hours offered. What they didn't know was that that was how she could afford Margurite.

"Where is it this time, Margo?" asked Tom, her co-worker. He had witnessed this phenomenon many times over the years. In fact, Tom had been one of the perpetuators of the urban legend of Margo.

"Bangkok," Margo answered. "I'm standing by on United out of San Francisco. The flight looks pretty open. Hopefully, I'll get on in first class. I'm staying at the Shangri-La. They're giving a great airline rate right now."

Over the years, Tom had gleaned enough information to enhance the legend by discovering that Margo went first class on these trips. She always took a suite in a five-star hotel, ate in the finest restaurants, and enjoyed top entertainment. It had taken him a long time to gain her trust and discover just this little bit about her "other" life. What Tom didn't know was that Margo knew about the legend, and she was, in fact, not upset by it. She was maybe even a bit amused. She had not, of course, shared her biggest secret. A secret she couldn't know had taken a profound toll, consuming energies that might have otherwise been put to building a happy life.

CHAPTER 3

November 1978

Rick and Margo met in the early days of her career when she transferred to Los Angeles from Seattle. It was the fresh start she needed after the breakup from Johnny. There was a wholesomeness about this twenty-two-year-old. Her flawless, ivory skin stood out in contrast to her sun-tanned California co-workers. Her soft brown eyes seemed to always be smiling. Beyond her looks, people were drawn in by her friendliness and expertise. She always seemed able to put a smile on a customer's face even under difficult circumstances, and her co-workers appreciated being able to ask her for assistance when they couldn't resolve an issue.

Rick was her boss. Everyone liked him. He had an easy, friendly but firm way about him. He always had his employees' backs. If they made a mistake, he would take the blame then have the much needed "talk" in private. The employees admired this about him, and even looked up to him like an older brother they didn't want to disappoint. Many times, his airport group was cited for exemplary service. It was widely rumored that Rick would move up the ladder quickly.

It happened at the annual Christmas party as it often does. The pleasantries of the workplace turned to recognition of what had been simmering between them.

"Are you enjoying yourself?" Rick asked, sliding onto the barstool next to her and leaning in. "L.A. must be a big change from Seattle."

"It is but I like it. I really like the people here and working for you," Margo could smell his aftershave. It stirred something in her. *His eyes are so blue. Cobalt blue. I hadn't noticed that before.* Of course, she had noticed his good looks the first time she saw him. The women she worked with called him Robert Redford.

"What do you think of our Robert Redford boss?" they teased when she first arrived.

It was rather disconcerting when she had to talk to him at work but now, in this festive atmosphere, he was just a handsome guy sitting next to her being nice. A shock of blonde hair fell across his brow. Margo resisted the temptation to brush it back ala Barbra Streisand in her favorite movie, *The Way We Were.* She felt the warmth creep up her neck and onto her cheeks. She took a big gulp of her vodka tonic.

"I know when I came here from Denver, it was quite a culture shock," he went on. "But I'm getting used to it, and I love the job."

Margo had heard the rumors about his "golden boy" status with the higher-ups. He had been promoted to his current position a year earlier, and would probably be moving on to a regional position soon. But all of that was not on her mind as she listened to his warm voice telling her about living in L.A.; all the while trying to be charming without flirting. She was glad she had chosen to wear her slightly off-the-shoulder, red silk dress. She was feeling lonely on her first Christmas in a new city without her old boyfriend. This dress always boosted her confidence.

"Are you okay to drive?" Rick asked, as he walked her to her car.

"I'm fine, thanks. It was a nice party. I enjoyed talking to you. See you at work."

As he reached over to open her car door, his cheek brushed hers.

"Merry Christmas, I'm glad you're here," he said, his voice husky, his breath warm and smelling of cognac. "You look lovely, by the way."

Margo slid into the seat quickly, and fumbled to get her keys in the ignition.

"I'm glad I'm here, too. Merry Christmas."

She didn't know why she didn't move away when Rick leaned in and kissed her cheek before he closed her door. She would look back on that night with pleasure and pain; the night she gave herself the Christmas gift of an affair with her married boss.

As she had every Tuesday and Thursday night, Margo sat on her comfy, floral print sofa flanked by matching faux marble-topped end tables, and waited for the arrival of her lover. But this night, the usual pleasurable fluttering in her stomach and tingling anticipation were replaced by anxiety. She busied herself fluffing the lemon yellow and lime green throw pillows, and flipping through the *Glamour* and *Cosmopolitan* magazines on the glass-topped coffee table.

At first, Margo had told herself he wasn't happy at home but the truth was Rick never talked about his wife, and certainly never complained or led her to believe he might leave his marriage. Their attraction was overwhelming. They were careful not to be alone together at work, and always spoke to each other in a professional way. In her apartment, as they lay in bed after making love, he would talk to her about his future plans, how much he loved the company, and his work. Margo learned from her co-workers that Rick's wife was known as the perfect hostess—an important skill needed to support her husband's career. He was already on the third rung of the corporate ladder, and she was his partner in reaching his goals. Margo dreamt about what it would be like to be married to Rick. They could travel the world. He had shared with her that early in their marriage his wife was diagnosed with endometriosis that left her unable to bear children. He was so wrapped up in his career she wondered if he even wanted children.

When Rick appeared at the door of Margo's apartment, he was waving a bottle of champagne.

"What are we celebrating?" she laughed, though she felt a little sick in her stomach. She knew he was about to confirm the rumors.

"I got it, Kitt," Rick said. Because he called her Miss Kitteridge at work, he had begun calling her Kitt in private. "They're going to announce it tomorrow. I just came from the meeting. I'm going to be the regional manager over the Northwest and Canada!"

He put the bottle down on her entry table, grabbed her, and, swinging her around, planted a kiss on her lips.

"That's wonderful. You've worked so hard for it. You deserve it. So I guess you'll be moving to Seattle," she said, not really wanting to hear him say it.

"Yes, and you can come up, and show me your city."

"Sure, it'll be fun," she said, but she knew she wouldn't be showing him Seattle. *This is good. You know it isn't going anywhere. This is what he wants and this way, I won't have to find out if he would choose me. Maybe it isn't true.* After all, she hadn't seen the doctor yet.

"I'll get the glasses. You open the champagne. I'm so proud of you."

CHAPTER 4

It helped not seeing Rick every day. Busy settling into his new position and moving into his new home in Seattle, he called her less and less. The last time they had sex was the night before his going away party. It was bittersweet. She tried not to cling too tightly afterward. She didn't want to acknowledge what they both knew—this was the last time.

"It's too bad you couldn't come," her co-workers told her the next day. "It was a great party. Are you feeling better?"

She hadn't been able to face meeting Rick's wife or watch him celebrate knowing it was the end of their romance.

Now, she sat on the exam table swinging her legs nervously as the doctor returned to the room.

"You're going to have a baby," he said brightly. "You're about eight weeks along."

"What? I'm sorry, did you say eight weeks? That's wonderful," she said, feigning happiness while inside the panic set in.

She was in a fog as she left the doctor's office armed with pamphlets, a prescription for pre-natal vitamins, and a card bearing her next appointment date.

It was all she could do to keep from calling Rick and telling him about the baby. Instead, she called her best friend Kathy.

"I just came from the doctor. Kath, I'm pregnant!" Margo began sobbing.

There was a long pause on the other end. "How far along are you?" asked Kathy, her voice barely audible.

"Eight weeks. Oh my God, what am I going to do?"

"Have you told Rick?"

"Not yet. I don't know what to do. I'm afraid to tell him."

"Do you want him to marry you? Will he leave his wife?"

"I don't know. I knew it was wrong to get involved with a married man. You warned me. He never promised me anything." Margo blew her nose. "Honestly, I don't want to know whether he'll choose me over his wife. He was my boss. His whole life and career could be ruined. I'll be seen as 'the other woman'. We'll both lose our jobs over this; not to mention, the scandal of it all," she said, her voice rising.

"So, what are you going to do? Are you going to keep it?"

"I could never have an abortion!" The thought horrified her. "But I'm not ready to be a mother either. I'm only twenty-three. How can I raise a child on my own? Can you imagine what my sister will say?" Margo began to sob again.

"First of all, you're still in shock. This isn't the time to make any big decisions. Do you want me to come down there?"

"Could you? I hate to ask you, but I need you to help me decide what to do. I'm off this weekend."

"I'll take the red-eye Friday night. You can pick me up after work."

"Thank you so much."

"It'll be okay," Kathy said, trying to calm her. "We'll figure something out."

"Thanks so much, Kath, for being such a good friend." *Is this my punishment for having an affair with a married man? If mother were alive, she'd insist I go to confession. How could I have been so stupid?*

As soon as she picked Kathy up at the airport, Margo felt better.

"Have you decided what you're going to do?"

"I've made such a mess of things. At first, I couldn't believe that such a gorgeous, successful man could be attracted to me. I've only been with Johnny. I never meant to fall in love with him. He never promised me anything, and I thought that was enough for me. If I tell him I'm pregnant, I'll have to let him have a say in my decision. I don't want to make him choose me over his wife and career. Honestly, I'm afraid of what he'll choose."

"It sounds like you've already decided what you're going to do."

"I guess I have. Now what?"

"First, you're going to stop and get us some Rocky Road."

"I need to take a leave of absence," Margo said as she sat in Rick's old office talking to her new manager. "My aunt is sick, and I'm the only family she has," she lied. "I need to go and help her."

"That's too bad. I'm so sorry. I don't need to tell you we'll miss you. You're one of our best agents. Rick spoke very highly of you."

"Thank you. I think I should probably plan on taking six months. Hopefully, that will be enough to get her back to where she can be alone. I'll let you know if it goes longer." *If I ask for eight or nine months, he might guess my secret.*

While her older sister, Anne, was happy when Margo first moved close to her in L.A., her life was so busy with her lawyer husband, Richard, and their new son, Eric, they hadn't seen much of each other. Anne had always viewed the world in black and white. She was good at making a plan and following it. She met Richard in college, and settled into her role of supporting her up-and-coming young law student husband. It paid off; now she was enjoying the life of a successful junior partner's wife.

"Why can't you be more like Anne?" her mother would ask. "You've always got your head in the clouds. Think seriously about what you want your life to be like and plan for it like your sister."

After years of trying to measure up to Anne, Margo gave up her efforts to please them. She knew if she told her about the baby, she would have to endure Anne's judgment along with a recounting of the bad choices she always made. She could imagine her reaction: "An affair with your boss, and a married man at that? Now you're pregnant? Oh, Margo, how could you have been so stupid?"

Oh yes, Margo knew how that conversation would go.

The accident that took both her parents four years ago had been devastating but she had to admit she was relieved that she didn't have to tell her mother about her latest bad choice.

The next day Margo met Anne for lunch. She had practiced her story so that she had the proper level of enthusiasm. She kept her hands in her lap so Anne wouldn't see them trembling.

"I have to tell you, I'm excited about a new assignment for the company," she began. "They're sending me to our major destinations to train the ticket agents on customer service. I'll be away from L.A. for a few months but I'm honored they chose me. I'll be based in Denver so I'll need to give up my apartment. I'm going to store my stuff. It's a good thing you have mom's things," she said, trying to push down her resentment over that.

"Well, we'll miss you but I'm proud of you," Anne said, turning her attention to the menu, "What are you going to have?"

CHAPTER 5

For someone accustomed to flying, it felt like the first time. The unpredictability of the morning sickness she was experiencing made Margo anxious as she buckled her seatbelt. She had witnessed air sickness in others, and didn't relish being "that" person puking into the little white bag.

After talking it over with Kathy, Margo had decided to give the baby up for adoption. Kathy found her a place in Denver where she could await the birth of her child. Because Margo's mother had been a devout Catholic, the only stipulation Margo gave Kathy was that she didn't want to go to a home for unwed mothers that was run by the Catholic Church. She couldn't bear the judgment of a bunch of nuns reminding her of her sinful nature. She didn't want to think about how disappointed her mother would be. At first, Kathy encouraged her to come to a place in Seattle so she could help her but the thought of being in the same town as the father of her child was too overwhelming. She had resisted calling or writing to Rick until now and didn't want to risk weakening her resolve. She made a list of pros and cons. The cons always outweighed the pros. Still, it would have been comforting to have his support. She found herself resenting his absence until she reminded herself that Rick didn't even know he was about to become a father. *Maybe I should have given him a chance to choose me. No, I'm not ready to raise a child with, or without, the father.* Then the shame and guilt swept over her like the morning sickness. She reached up and rang the call button. *Maybe some Coca-Cola would help.*

The place in Denver was a modest two-story brick house on a tree-lined street. The porch steps were flanked by beds of purple iris and yellow tulips. A small sign by the door read, 'Welcome to Blair House'. The taxi driver followed Margo up the steps and placed her bag by the door. When she handed him his tip, she thought he gave her a knowing look as he turned, and walked down the sidewalk to his cab. Before she could ring the bell, a short, matronly woman opened the door, and peered through the screen.

"Miss Kitteridge? Welcome. My name is Mae Howard." She opened the screen door wide and reached for Margo's suitcase.

"It's okay. I can get it," Margo said, lifting the suitcase and stepping into the foyer.

Mae Howard wore a white cotton dress printed with little red cherries. She wiped her hands on a blue denim apron with a ruffled border. Her graying hair was pulled back in a neat bun at the nape of her neck. The smell of chocolate chip cookies filled the air. Margo was immediately transported to her grandmother's kitchen.

"I was just baking some cookies. Let's get you settled in your room, and you can join me in the kitchen for some tea. How does that sound?"

The buttercup yellow walls with pecan colored crown molding and baseboards gave the house a cozy feeling. Mae led Margo down the hall to the third bedroom on the right. It had wallpaper dotted with pink rosebuds. The comforter on the single bed was pink and white striped with a solid pink flounce. A white dresser and a dusty rose upholstered easy chair by the window completed the room.

"We have four bedrooms on this floor. The three in the front here are for you girls. Mine is in the back off the kitchen. You girls will share this bathroom," Mae said gesturing toward the door beside Margo's room. "There are three more bedrooms upstairs. Those girls will arrive tomorrow. Jane and Lily are in the living room watching television. Come let me introduce you."

Margo was dismayed to see that Jane and Lily were barely teenagers. Jane wore a sleeveless A-line orange cotton dress that bulged from her ample baby bump. Lily wore what Margo assumed were maternity leggings covered by a hot pink, slouchy sweatshirt. They both wore jelly shoes, the preferred fashion of the day.

"Girls, this is Margo. She'll be in the room at the end of the hall."

"Hello, I'm Jane. This is Lily."

Jane attempted to raise her bulky body out of the easy chair; but Margo reached down to shake her hand. "Don't get up, please." She walked over to the other chair to shake Lily's hand but withdrew it when Lily mumbled a hello and turned her attention back to the soap opera. *All My Children. How appropriate,* Margo mused. *I'll probably be the oldest one here. I'm sure I'll have nothing in common with any of these girls except that I'm having a baby without a husband.*

Are you ready for some tea and cookies?" Mae called from the kitchen.

Margo lay in bed that night and wondered, for the umpteenth time, how she got here. What had she been thinking when she started the affair with Rick? She really did love him. A part of her had hoped he'd want a future with her. Little did she know this was that future,—lying in a house in Denver counting rosebuds on the wallpaper. She turned out the lamp beside the bed. Just as she began to drift off to sleep, she felt movement. Placing her hand on her belly, she began to cry softly for the future she'd never have and the baby she couldn't keep.

The next day, one by one, the other girls arrived. Margo was relieved to see that at least one of them, the pudgy blonde Judy, was closer to her in age.

To keep them active and occupied, Mae Howard assigned them chores. They were responsible for the orderliness of their own rooms. They rotated bathroom duty, laundry, vacuuming, and dusting the common areas. Everyone helped at meal time from food preparation to setting the table and doing the dishes. In the evenings after supper, they could watch TV until the late-night news. Sometimes they played games, and on the weekends, some family members would visit.

Kathy told Margo she wanted to be with her when the baby was born. Since it was her first pregnancy, Margo insisted the date was too unpredictable, and she didn't want Kathy to miss work. When Kathy insisted that she at least fly back to L.A. with her after the baby was born, Margo gratefully agreed.

She didn't have much in common with most of the girls. All they talked about was boys and how they thought the father of their baby really loved them. Sara and Hannah were from very religious families who sent them to Blair House to cover up the pregnancies and preserve their standing in their church. Whatever they did, they did together, and they cried a lot.

One evening, Judy came to Margo's room after supper and plopped down on the end of her bed. "It seems we're a bit more mature than our roommates," she quipped. "Care to swap stories about how we got here?"

Not surprisingly, their stories were similar. Judy had also fallen in love with a married man. Although he wasn't her boss, it was even more scandalous. She was in the church choir and he was the choir director. When she found out she was pregnant, she left the choir and the church.

"It's such a classic story. I can't believe I let it happen to me," Judy said. "I had broken up with my long-term boyfriend, and it was so comforting to have Ray to talk with. Before long, the friendly hug ended in a kiss and the rest is history. I knew it was wrong but I couldn't stop myself. I told myself he loved me but when I told him about the baby, I knew he didn't. He said he'd pay for me to go somewhere to have the baby as long as I agreed to keep it quiet and give it up for adoption."

From then on, Margo and Judy formed a bond. Somehow it helped Margo to know she wasn't the only person stupid enough to put herself in this predicament at her age.

The night her water broke, they were in the living room watching a very pregnant Lucille Ball in an *I Love Lucy* rerun. Margo had become more and more uncomfortable as the day went on so laughing at Ricky Ricardo racing out the door with Lucy's bag minus Lucy took her mind off the ache in her lower back. She would recall later how ironic it was that Ricky left Lucy behind, and her own Rick wasn't with her when Mae Howard called the Blair House nurse to accompany Margo to the hospital.

The lady from the adoption agency told Margo it would be best for her not to see her baby after it was born so she was surprised when a nurse entered the room, and laid a tiny bundle in her arms. She moved the blanket back from her baby girl's face and stared into Rick's eyes. She had a full head of dark hair and Margo's long eyelashes. *She's so precious. Maybe I can do this. Maybe I can raise her by myself. Maybe if Rick knew about her, saw her, he would want to be with us.*

The nurse scurried back into the room. Her face was beet red.

"I'm sorry. It'll be all right, honey," the nurse said, leaning down and taking the baby from Margo. "The couple who are adopting her are very nice and very excited to take her home. You're doing the right thing, honey." Just like that, her baby was gone.

"Thank you, Kath, for coming out to fly home with me," Margo said, as she fastened her seatbelt. "You were right. I needed you here."

"I'm glad to do it. When are you going back to work? When is your leave up?" Kathy asked.

"I've decided I can't go back to working at the airport. I don't know how good I'd be at lying to those nice people. Besides, I'd rather not be working in Rick's division. I'm putting in for a position in Reservations, preferably the night shift. I'll stay in a hotel until I can find an apartment. By the time the position is available, I should no longer look like I ate my way through the leave of absence."

She sold the furniture she had stored. She didn't want to be reminded of that time in her life. She didn't want to sit on the sofa where they enjoyed a glass of wine together and talked about their day. She couldn't sleep in the bed where they had made love. The bed where her baby, the baby she gave up, was conceived.

She found a one-bedroom apartment near the airport and the company headquarters and furnished it with the bare necessities. She had no desire to make it a home; she only needed a place to sleep which was all she seemed to do these days.

As planned, she went to work on the night shift in Reservations. She didn't need to wear a uniform or bother about her hair or makeup and that suited her just fine. She kept to herself. Something in her made her feel they wouldn't like her if they knew what she'd done. She liked that she could still solve problems for her customers, but she didn't have to see them face to face. Working problems out for them was a distraction she badly needed. Leaving work in the early morning hours kept her from seeing too many people. All she wanted to do was go home and sleep, but sometimes that was difficult because of the dreams. She kept seeing her baby's face and then the nurse taking her away. She would awaken to a damp pillow and a heart pounding so hard she could hear it. Rarely, she would awaken with a feeling of joy when, in her dream, she had her baby back. That dream was worse because the joy quickly turned to depression when she realized it wasn't true. *I did what was best for her. I could never be the mother she deserves.*

When she had lost the baby weight, Margo made a lunch date with her sister, Anne. She wasn't looking forward to it. She knew she couldn't be the old Margo or she might weaken and tell her the whole story. Besides, she didn't feel like that Margo anymore. That was the day she created her alter ego Margurite, a more confident version of Margo, to conceal her anxiety. She bought a red-and-white polka dot sundress and white patent-leather pumps. A straw purse, a necklace of white beads and bright cherry-red lipstick completed Margurite's look. Anne was already seated at a table by a window. Margurite strode confidently to the table and leaned down to give Anne a peck on the cheek she offered.

"You look different," Anne said. "Much better than when you left. Have you lost weight? The time away from your routine and the special assignment has done you good. You must tell me all about it. What are you going to have? I think I'll have the club but I suppose you're sticking to salads these days."

And there it is. Anne giveth and Anne taketh away.

That day when she got home, she put Margurite back on the clothes rack in her bedroom and didn't bring her out again until she went on vacation.

CHAPTER 6

The feeling of loss, the mourning over her child and the pain of what she had done increased as the years went by. The suppressed guilt eroded her self-image. Quite unexpectedly, it would seep into her consciousness and she was aware she was hiding something. It began to impact her daily living. She stopped showering regularly, brushing her hair or wearing clean clothes. Some days she struggled to get out of bed and go to work. She wasn't fond of who she had become and believed that others could see the "damned spot" she couldn't wash out.

Every time she saw a girl with dark hair who would be about her child's age, she wondered what she was doing, whether she was happy, and what her parents were like. *What did they name her?* It was especially difficult on her daughter's birthdays. *Did she know she was adopted? What did she know about her birth mother? Had they told her she was dead?* That thought horrified her. Margo wished she could tell her that she gave her up so she could have a better life than the one she could have given her.

Whenever these thoughts began to overwhelm her, she would call Kathy.

"Hi Kath, how are you guys doing?" she asked half-heartedly.

"We're doing okay but you don't sound so good, what's going on? Still having those dreams?"

"I'm such a terrible person. Did I make a mistake?" she sobbed.

"Honey," Kathy soothed, "you did what was best for your baby. Back then, it would have been very difficult for you to work and take care of her. Like you said, you probably would have lost your job. You were so young. Do you want me to come down and see you?"

"No, I'll be all right. I just needed to talk to you."

Over the years, Margo and Kathy stayed in touch but Margo never let Kathy come visit her. She knew Kathy would be upset to see where and how she lived, and who she had become. Whenever they did get together, it was Margurite who flew up to Seattle.

January 1998

When her daughter turned eighteen, Margo decided she needed to know what happened to the baby she had given up. She didn't quite know how to go about finding her. Her sister Anne's boy, Eric, was the only person she could think of who might be able to help. Margo had poured her love on him after she gave up her baby. However, as time went on, it became harder and harder for Margo to watch him grow wondering how her own child was doing, so she stopped visiting them.

In their annual Christmas letter, Anne enclosed a photo of the family and bragged about Eric graduating from college and interning at the courthouse while attending law school. Now, as Margo sat on a bench outside the courthouse, she was able to recognize him as he passed.

"Eric?" she called out.

Eric walked back to the bench. "Yes, do I know you?"

Margo rose, lifted her head and looked deeply into his eyes. "I'm your Aunt Margo. Can we talk?"

"Aunt Margo? What's happened to you?" His face flushed. "I mean, are you okay?"

Eric reached out to hug her but she stepped back. She knew she must seem dirty.

"Do you have time to talk?"

"I, I guess so. I'm on my lunch hour. Can I buy you a hot dog? We can go to the park over there," he said, gesturing across the courtyard.

"That'll be fine. But let me buy our hot dogs," she said fumbling in her zebra print fanny pack that hung loosely over one hip.

"That's okay. I'll get it. You go get us a bench. What do you want on your dog? Anything to drink?"

"Just mustard and a small cola, thanks."

Margo sat on the park bench watching Eric approach balancing their lunch in the cardboard carrier. *How do I begin?*

"Eric, I know you must be surprised to see me after all this time but I need your help."

"It has been a long time, Aunt Margo, what can I do? Do you need money, a place to stay?" Eric asked gently, sitting down and placing their lunch on the bench between them.

"No, I'm fine. I know I must not look like it but I'm fine." She took a sip of her drink. "First, I need you to keep what I'm about to tell you a secret. You can't tell anyone, especially your mother."

Eric leaned forward, intrigued. "I promise."

Margo placed her drink in the cardboard container, and folded her hands in her lap. She fixed her eyes on them, not wanting to see Eric's reaction to what she was about to say.

"Eighteen years ago, I had a child. A little girl. The father doesn't know. He was married. I was only twenty-three, not ready to be a mother or take care of a baby. I decided not to tell him and instead gave her up for adoption." Margo glanced up at Eric and rushed on. "I've thought about her all these years. I want to find her. I want to know if she's all right. I don't want her to know I'm looking for her and I don't want to meet her," Margo added quickly.

Eric took her hands in his. "I'm so sorry, Aunt Margo. Of course, I'll help. Let's see, I'll need to get the name of the agency you used, the date, and the hospital where she was born. Some of the laws about adoption information have changed so that might help us."

"Thank you, Eric," she said, wiping the tears from her cheek with the back of her hand.

They agreed to meet the following week for another hot dog lunch in the park outside the courthouse. She said it was easier than meeting him at a restaurant. She knew how it would look, a nice young man taking pity on a homeless bag lady. Maybe someday she would introduce him to Margurite. Margurite would love to dine with him in a fine restaurant. He would even be her guest.

When they met again, Eric had some news for Margo. As they sat on their bench, he took her hands in his.

"I found her," he said. "Her name is Aimee Gordon. She was adopted by an upper middle-class couple and raised in Ventura. I'm sorry that's all I could find out," he searched her face as he spoke. "Do you want to try to meet her?"

Margo's eyes misted over as she fumbled in her fanny pack for a tissue. Dabbing at the tears welling up, she realized Eric was looking at her, deep concern in his eyes. "No, I just wanted to know if she had a good home, that I did the right thing giving her up. I thought she would still be in Colorado and not so close."

"If you decide you want to see her, I'd be happy to help with that. I would even go with you to meet her."

"I don't know. I'll have to think about it." Margo wasn't sure she was ready to share her secret and face the shame she felt. She choked back a sob and patted his hand, "It's okay, Eric, you've done a great job just getting that much information. Are you free tomorrow night? I'd like to take you to dinner for all the time you put into this."

"You don't have to do that, Aunt Margo. I'm happy I could help."

"It will be my pleasure and I won't embarrass you," Margo said, noticing the tips of his ears turn red. "Tomorrow night, seven o'clock, at Oceans in Santa Monica? I want you to meet Margurite."

"Who's Margurite?"

"Just wait. I think you'll like her."

CHAPTER 7

When Margo entered the restaurant, she was aware of the admiring glances of the men at the bar. She always felt empowered when she took on the persona of Margurite. She wore a long-sleeved, black Michael Kors dress with a V-neckline and shirring that nipped in at her narrow waist, releasing the silk fabric over her hips in a slight flare. She had swept her wavy hair up on one side and clipped it with a silver butterfly pin. She seemed to glide across the floor in her crystal-studded black pumps. She was, in a word, stunning.

As the *maître d* escorted her to the table, Eric rose, stumbling and nearly knocking over his chair. His eyes were wide.

"Hello, Eric. I'm Margurite," Margo said, smiling mischievously as she extended her hand to greet him.

Eric pulled out her chair. After she was seated, he fairly fell into his.

"Aunt Margo, uh sorry, Margurite, you look lovely."

"Thanks dear. Don't worry; you can still call me Aunt Margo. Whatever you prefer," she laughed softly. "I know this comes as a shock but I told you I wouldn't embarrass you."

"I don't understand, Aunt Margo. Why aren't you like this all the time?"

"It's complicated, Eric. You know a little about my past and about Aimee. After giving up my baby, I guess I just stopped caring about anything. At first, I felt sorry for myself. I even blamed the father who didn't know I was pregnant. I fantasized about telling him. I imagined him leaving his wife, finding our child, and living happily ever after. But it was too late for that. I'm to blame. I'm the one who has to live with my decision. All I do is go to work, go home, and retreat into my books. I'm afraid you saw the result of that when you met me in the park. I'm sure you thought I was some homeless person."

She reached over and patted his hand before he could protest.

"It's okay. The first time Margurite appeared was when I returned from having the baby and I had to meet your mother for lunch. You know how intimidating she can be." Eric rolled his eyes and nodded understandingly. "Becoming Margurite helped me be confident enough to ensure I didn't feel the need to share my secret."

"Wow, so mom is responsible for my lovely dinner date," he said, grinning.

"I guess you could say that," Margo said, smiling at the thought. "Now when I need to meet the company dress code to get on a plane, it's always Margurite who does the travelling. You could say she's my alter ego, but she doesn't have any superpowers."

"But why do you go back to being Margo?" Eric asked softly, intrigued but not wanting to offend her.

"I don't know. After what I did, I guess I feel I don't deserve to be Margurite all the time. Margo is who I really am now. But enough of that," she said, turning her attention to the approaching waiter. "What would you like to eat? My treat. How about a glass of wine to toast all your hard work?"

"I'll say one thing, Aunt Margo, uh Margurite, I see a lot of jealous men in here eyeing my glamorous companion," teased Eric.

CHAPTER 8

That dinner last week with Eric was on her mind as Margo dressed for work as well as the meeting with the police in the morning. *Maybe Margurite should be the one to go,* she thought. *After all, I am going as Aimee's mother.* It was the first time in a long time she actually cared about what others might think, but she had to go straight from work. If she showed up as Margurite, there would be questions from her co-workers, especially Tom. Instead, she showered, put on a clean T-shirt, and pulled her hair up in a ponytail.

In the morning when Margo arrived at the police station, she realized she had never been in one before; it made her nervous. The precinct looked like the ones she had seen in the cop shows on television. There were rows of gray metal desks manned by men of all ages, sizes, and ethnicities. Most were dressed in dark suits, white shirts, and striped ties with only a few in uniform or jeans and T-shirts. Phones were ringing. The dingy green walls were bare, with the exception of a large bulletin board pinned with flyers announcing "Wanted" or "Missing". Margo wondered if one of the young girls on the posters could be her daughter. She shivered.

"I'm Margo Kitteridge. I'm here to see Detective Carpenter," Margo said to the officer behind the counter.

He glanced up and balancing the phone on his shoulder, pointed with his right hand.

"The corner office over there."

Margo headed down the hallway and tapped on the open door. Detective Carpenter sat at a large desk covered with case files.

"Miss Kitteridge? Detective Sam Carpenter," he said, rising and leaning over his desk to greet her. "Thank you for coming. Please, sit down."

Margo was immediately struck by his good looks. Although he was clean-shaven, Detective Carpenter looked like he had come right out of central casting for *Magnum P.I.* When he sat down, his broad shoulders overflowed the leather chair.

Margo sat stiffly in the chair in front of his desk. "Please, Detective Carpenter, tell me about Aimee. What kind of trouble is she in?"

"As I told you on the phone, Aimee disappeared a few days ago. Her parents, uh, her adoptive parents, gave us your name as her birth mother. They found out from her friend that she was searching for you. They thought maybe she had contacted you or might be with you."

"No, I haven't seen or heard from her. I had started searching for her too. I just needed to know how she was doing. You know, who adopted her, and what kind of life she was living." Margo shifted in her chair. "You said she's in trouble. What kind of trouble?"

"Miss Kitteridge…"

"Margo, please."

"Margo, it appears she's run away and we have reason to believe she may be caught up in a sex trafficking operation."

Margo sucked in her breath and leaned forward. "What? Oh God, how can that be? What makes you think that?"

"I'm part of a team assigned to investigate human trafficking, sex trafficking, in the city. Whenever a young girl like Aimee goes missing, we're notified. Recently, we raided a house where some girls were reportedly being kept. Aimee wasn't there, but two of the girls identified her from a photo as having been at the house. They said she was with a good-looking young man who spoke in a foreign language to one of the men and then they left. I'm sorry, I know this is a lot to take in."

"Oh my God!" Margo slumped back in the chair, tears welled in the corners of her eyes. She fumbled for a tissue in her fanny pack.

"I'm so sorry," Sam said, extending a tissue box.

Margo grabbed two tissues and quickly dabbed at her eyes.

"I wish she had contacted me. Maybe I could have..." her voice trailed off into a stifled sob.

"Margo, we're working very hard to find out what happened to her," Sam said gently. "If she does get in touch with you, here's my card with my number on it. Call me at any time, day or night. Now, can I get some information from you? You came here from work. Where do you work? I'll need your work number."

As Margo answered Sam's questions, she noted he seemed surprised to learn she was employed and not homeless. He stole quick glances at her.

"Is that all you need?"

"Yes, yes, that's fine for now. I'll keep in touch. Call me immediately if you hear anything or think of anything that might help."

"I will. Thank you, Detective Carpenter. And please keep me informed."

He rose and shook Margo's hand. "Call me Sam. I'll be in touch."

Driving home, questions raged in Margo's brain. *Why would Aimee run away? Was she abused? Who is this foreign man she's with? Is she being abused and raped right now? I shouldn't have given her up. Where is she, my sweet baby girl?* Tears began rolling down her face. *I have to call Kathy and Eric.*

CHAPTER 9

Margo decided to call in sick. She knew she wouldn't be able to concentrate on anything. That night she had another one of her dreams, or rather a nightmare. Everything around her was white. She was lying in a hospital bed. Cuddled in the crook of her arm was her new baby girl. A dark figure entered the room. It was a nurse.

"I'm sorry. It'll be all right, honey," the nurse said, leaning down and taking the baby from Margo. "The couple who are adopting her are very nice and very excited to take her home. You're doing the right thing, honey."

When the nurse left, another dark figure entered the room. At first, she thought it was Rick but it was Detective Sam Carpenter.

"Margo, where's Aimee? I thought you said she was with you and you were taking care of her. I've been looking everywhere for her. What have you done with her?" he asked accusingly. Suddenly, his face turned into Rick's.

She tried to cry out and tell him they had taken their baby away, but she couldn't make any sound. Margo turned her head away and dissolved in tears.

The shrill ring of the telephone startled her awake. Her heart was racing; her face and pillow were wet with her tears.

"Margo, so what happened at the police station?" Kathy asked. "I'm sorry I didn't get back to you yesterday, but we got home too late to call before you went to work."

"I didn't go to work last night. I was too upset."

"Why? What did they tell you?"

"Kath, Aimee's adoptive parents told Detective Carpenter that Aimee might be looking for me," Margo began to choke up. "They thought she might have contacted me or she might even be with me. I told him I was looking for her, but I hadn't tried to contact her."

"Oh, my God, she was looking for you too?"

"They think she might have been taken by a sex trafficking ring!"

"What?" Kathy exclaimed. "How horrible! What makes them think that?"

"They raided a house where some young girls were being held. When they showed them a picture of Aimee, one of the girls recognized her and said she was there with some guy who spoke in a foreign language to one of the men and then they left."

"Oh, my God, I can't believe this."

"I need to find out about sex trafficking. I'm going to ask Eric to do some research. You know, how does it happen? Who's involved? How can someone get out? I only know a little about it from my travels to Bangkok. It's a big part of the tourist trade there. Can you believe it?"

"I've read a little about it in the newspaper. I know it's mostly been in Asia, but lately there have been reports that it's happening more and more here in the States. It's really sickening."

"Detective Carpenter gave me his card. He said he'd stay in touch and to call him if I hear from Aimee or think of any information that could help them." Margo's voice faltered. "I'm so scared for her. I wish she had found me. Maybe I could have stopped this from happening. Maybe if I hadn't given her up."

"None of this is your fault. Let's focus on seeing her being found unharmed. You know what I always say about putting bad thoughts out into the universe."

"I know. Thanks, Kath. I'll call you when I get more information."

CHAPTER 10

SAM

Detective Carpenter studied the copy of Aimee Gordon's picture. Aimee had the same dark lashes as Margo, but unlike her mother, her eyes were a striking shade of blue. She smiled up at him, her head cocked a little to one side—a pose typical of high school pictures. He wondered what had happened in Aimee's home to make her run away. When he interviewed her adoptive parents, there was no indication of abuse. He knew that teenagers rebelled so he was going with that assumption. She fit the profile of a child of privilege—her father a successful banker and her mother serving on various community boards and charitable committees. He knew Aimee had traveled with them. She had a passport and, at the moment, that was the only available tool for their investigation. They were tracking its possible use through Customs at the airports and ports, but Sam didn't hold out much hope. He knew if Aimee was in the hands of a human trafficking ring, they would use fake passports to move their victims.

Since Margo worked for an airline, Sam wasn't surprised that she had a passport. What surprised him was her passport picture. As he suspected that first day at the station, Margo was a very attractive woman under all that "bag lady" appearance. The resemblance to Aimee was apparent in the "spruced up" version of her smiling back at him. He noted that she had made frequent trips to Bangkok, a well-known base for sex trafficking; a city where Aimee's captors may have taken her. He picked up the phone.

"Hello, Miss Kitteridge, uh, Margo, this is Sam Carpenter from the LAPD."

"Yes, Detective Carpenter, do you have news about Aimee?" Margo asked anxiously.

"Nothing new but I would like to ask you some more questions. Are you available this afternoon?" He wanted to observe her facial expressions when he told her their working theory.

"I, I guess so. What time? Do you want me to come down to the station?"

"No, I'm going to be at the courthouse today. If you could meet me at the Coffee Grind around the corner on Fifth Street, I'll buy you a cup of coffee. Believe me, it'll be better than the coffee at the station," Sam said, trying to lighten the mood. "How about two o'clock?"

"I can do that," Margo answered. "See you there."

Margo rummaged nervously through Margurite's clothes before she selected a pair of black skinny jeans, a royal blue T-shirt, and a black denim jacket. She limited her makeup to a little mascara and pink-tinted lip-gloss. Pulling her hair into a loose ponytail and slipping into low-heeled black suede boots, she glanced at her alter ego in the mirror.

Entering the Coffee Grind, Margo searched the room.

"Over here," Sam called rising and pulling out a chair for her. "Thank you for coming on such short notice."

Margo's cheeks flushed when she saw the look of admiration on his face as she approached the table.

"What can I get for you?"

"I'll have a small cup of their special blend with a splash of non-fat milk, please." As she said it, Margo realized she was definitely in Margurite mode.

She watched Sam stride to the counter; all six-feet-two of him. She admired the way the dark blue suit jacket stretched taut across his back. The white, button-down shirt and blue and gray striped tie seemed out of place on a body designed more for tight jeans and an equally tight T-shirt. *It's probably his court outfit. He's really attractive.* She realized she hadn't paid attention to a man's looks in a very long time.

As Sam delivered their coffee, he placed a plate with two delicious looking muffins in the middle of the table.

"One's blueberry and the other is spice. Take your pick."

"I'll take the spice, thanks. I know most guys like blueberry," she said, averting her eyes when she realized she might be flirting a little.

"Thanks for not making a joke about me preferring donuts," Sam grinned. "You know, since I'm a cop."

Margo let out a low laugh, relaxing for the first time in a long time. She liked the way his hazel eyes crinkled at the corners when he smiled. He leaned forward.

"Margo, it seems Aimee has had a good life with her adoptive parents. You might say a privileged life. She got to travel with them. One of those trips was to Bangkok. Are you aware that Bangkok is a well-known center for those involved in sex trafficking?" Sam went on, eyeing her reaction closely.

"I've heard that. I've visited there many times. It seems to be common knowledge among my friends there," Margo's eyes widened. "Oh, no, do you think that's where they've taken Aimee?"

"We don't have anything to indicate that right now, but we are tracking any activity on her passport. You say you've been to Bangkok many times to visit friends?"

"Yes, I started going a few years ago to visit a co-worker who transferred there. I fell in love with the city and the people. It seems so strange and awful to think it has this dark side to it."

"Unfortunately, in my line of work, I see mostly the dark side of humanity. When was the last time you were there?"

"About two months ago. Why?"

"I guess you can go pretty much anytime you want working for an airline."

"That's true," her eyes narrowed. *Why is he asking me that?*

"At the station, you said you had been looking for Aimee. What did you find out about her? You obviously knew her name, but you say you didn't contact her."

"No. I just wanted to know if she was having a good life. When I learned about her adoptive parents, it made me feel better; like I had done the right thing by giving her up." She looked Sam straight in his eyes. "Surely, you don't think I had anything to do with her disappearance. I would never do anything to hurt my child!"

Sam reached over and covered her hand with his then quickly withdrew it. "I'm sorry, but I have to ask these questions. It's my job." He reached into his breast pocket and pulled out a photocopy of Aimee's picture. "It occurred to me that if Aimee was hanging around your neighborhood or office trying to get up the courage to talk to you, you wouldn't even know it. Here's a copy of her high school graduation picture."

"Oh, she's so pretty," Margo said, running her hand over the photo. She looked up at Sam. "Oh God, I don't even want to think about what might be happening to her right now! I feel so helpless."

Sam leaned across the table. "I'm so sorry, Margo. I know this is really hard. I have a daughter about Aimee's age. I can't imagine what I'd do if she disappeared. Trust me, I'm doing all I can to find her."

"I know you are and I really appreciate it," Margo said, wiping a tear from her cheek with the back of her hand.

"Well, I'd better get back to the courthouse," Sam said, standing up. "I'll let you know if anything comes up. You can call me anytime."

"Thank you, Sam," she said. "Thank you for the picture."

"I'll be in touch," Sam said, patting her shoulder.

CHAPTER 11

AIMEE

Kris unlocked the door and motioned Aimee inside. As her eyes adjusted to the dimly-lit room, she could make out the outline of a sofa flanked by two overstuffed armchairs. Kris flipped the switch by the door, filling the room with a pale yellow light from the overhead fan. A small television sat on a table in one corner. Along one wall was an avocado-colored refrigerator next to a small counter with a white sink and stove. A round table with chrome legs and three matching chairs with red vinyl backs and seats divided the room. The concrete floor was painted brown. A beige, gold and brown striped rectangular rug stretched in front of the tan, faux leather sofa.

Aimee turned toward Kris. Her brow furrowed.

"I know it's not the Hilton but it's only for tonight," Kris said apologetically. The first night they had stayed in Kris's hotel suite. The next day they visited a house where Kris met some Thai friends who gave him the key to this place.

"The bedroom and bathroom are back here," he said, leading her through the archway off the living room. He sat her bag in the corner of the bedroom.

Aimee followed him back into the living room.

"I just have to check on the arrangements for our trip. Don't worry, I won't be gone long. I'll bring back a pizza." He leaned down and kissed her deeply. "Try to get some rest. It's going to be a long trip."

Aimee pulled the short red, brown and buttercream plaid curtains aside and watched the rental car pull away. The window had bars on it. They were the kind of bars she had seen on the little houses in South Los Angeles that still stood as a symbol of happier times before the neighborhood succumbed to crime and poverty. Originally, they were meant to be decorative, black wrought iron with pointed tops much like the fence around her home in Ventura. Now they were needed to protect the occupants of this house in this once sweet neighborhood.

Suddenly, Aimee felt panic tightening her chest. She rattled the door to be sure it was locked. *What am I doing here? I want to go home. Where is home?* Then she thought about Kris, how she felt at the hotel when he had made love to her. How he looked deeply into her eyes as though he really saw her. There was so much mystery about him. He took his time exploring her body. She wanted to do everything to please him. She didn't know sex could be like that. She didn't even mind that he pinned her arms down when he kissed her. It was exciting. She was his woman. He was in charge; not like the boys in school who were awkward and didn't really know what to do. But when she told him she had never gone all the way, he stopped.

"It's okay," he said, stroking her hair, "we can wait until we're married."

Entering the bedroom, she sat down on the edge of the bed and looked over at her Louis Vuitton travel bag in the corner. She had been so excited when she had packed it. It was all very romantic, running away with Kris. He was so foreign and yet so familiar. She loved him. She trusted him. He wouldn't lie to her like her parents had. She smiled remembering the trip to Thailand and the first time she saw him.

CHAPTER 12

It was a month before that trip when she found out. Aimee had been experiencing stomach pains after she ate. Sometimes the pain was so intense, she doubled over. After an initial exam, the doctor asked about family history.

"You go ahead and get dressed, Aimee," her mother said. "Let's step out, doctor, and I'll give you the information."

Curious, Aimee pressed her ear to the door.

"I'm sorry. I can't tell you much about Aimee's family history, doctor," Helen said, in a low voice. "She's adopted."

Aimee sucked in her breath and covered her mouth to stifle a cry. Her mind was racing. *Adopted? No wonder she sometimes felt like she didn't belong in her family. She didn't look like any of her cousins. Why hadn't her mother and father told her? Did she come from a bad mother? Did she inherit some horrible disease from her real mother? Was she some kind of addict? Who was her mother?*

When Helen returned to the room, Aimee was dressed. She pushed past her mother into the waiting room and out the door.

Fighting back tears, she rushed to the car, opened the door, slid in, and slammed it behind her. Helen scurried to catch up with her. She pulled the driver door open and quickly slid in.

"What's the matter, Aimee? Why didn't you wait for me?"

"I heard you tell the doctor I was adopted!" She half-yelled, half-sobbed. "Is it true? Am I adopted? Why didn't you tell me before now? Who are my real parents? Do I have some horrible hereditary disease?"

Stunned, Helen reached across the console to put her arms around her. Aimee flinched and pressed herself against the passenger door.

"Aimee, I'm so sorry you had to find out this way." Helen rushed on. "I can tell you there were no health issues with your birth mother. No drug or alcohol abuse."

"Then why did she give me up? Why didn't she want me?"

"She was young and single. The father wasn't in the picture. She loved you so much that she wanted you to have a good home with a mother and a father and she couldn't give you that. Aimee, I want you to know that you are my heart daughter. Your father and I have loved you as our own. We were living in Denver when we found out we couldn't have children. We waited a long time for the adoption agency to find you for us. Aimee, we always felt God sent you to us. Please believe me. Why, we even named you Aimee because it means 'Beloved.'"

"I was born in Colorado?"

"Yes, but we moved to Los Angeles when you were two months old so this has always been your home."

"Wow, what else don't I know about myself? Do you know who my birth mother is? Her name?"

"No, honey," Helen lied. "It was a closed adoption. I'm so sorry. We probably should have told you but there never seemed to be a right time."

"Are you sure I don't have something I got from her?" Aimee asked accusingly.

"The doctor is running all kinds of tests. I'm sure it will be okay. You were a very healthy baby. This is the first time you've had any real issues. Try not to worry. Whatever it is, I'm here for you. Aimee, please, I love you so much." Helen reached for Aimee again, but she pulled her arm away and looked out the window.

"I know, Mother," she replied icily.

When they arrived home, Aimee raced up the stairs to her room and called her best friend Debbie.

"Deb, can I come over right now? I need to talk to you."

"Sure, what's wrong? You sound upset."

"I am. I'll tell you when I get there."

She stumbled back down the stairs, struggling to put her sweater on.

"Aimee, where are you going?" Helen called from the kitchen.

"I'm going to Debbie's house," she said, slamming the front door.

When Debbie opened the door, Aimee dissolved into tears.

"Can we go to your room?"

"Of course, what's wrong?" Debbie asked, putting her arm around Aimee's shoulder and guiding her to the bedroom.

Aimee sank down on the bed and began to relate the scene at the doctor's office.

"Oh, Aimee, what a terrible way to find out you're adopted!" Debbie said. "Why didn't they tell you before this?"

"Mother said there was no good time. Now I wonder if there's something wrong with me that made my birth mother give me up. Mother says no but how can I believe anything she says?" She began to sob. Debbie handed her a Kleenex. "You know I'm nothing like my parents, especially Mother. She's tall and slender and you know I've always had trouble keeping my weight down." She blew her nose. "We were at the doctor to find out why I've been having these stomach cramps. Oh, Deb, what if I have some horrible hereditary disease?"

She fell back on the bed. Debbie lay down on her side facing Aimee.

"It'll be okay," she said, patting her shoulder. "What are you going to do now that you know?"

"I have to find out who my birth mother is and why she gave me up. I'm going to look for papers or some kind of information at the house. If I can find a birth certificate or adoption papers, I can try that new website where you can trace your ancestry. I can't let my parents know. I have to find out who I really am and where I come from." She turned on her side to look at Debbie. "You know, there's always been a part of me that felt like an outsider in our family. I don't look like any of my cousins. I'm just an average student. I can never meet my parents' expectations. They're planning for me to go to college and become some kind of professional. I'm afraid to tell them I have no interest in that." Aimee sat up pulling Debbie up with her. Her eyes widened. "I've always wanted to travel. Father travels all the time. Mother goes with him sometimes. I only got to go with them once when they went to Rome. I loved it. Maybe I could work for the airlines."

"That would be so cool." Debbie's brow furrowed. "But I thought we were going to be roomies at college."

"Go to work for the airlines with me. It'll be fun travelling all over the world together. You might meet a handsome pilot. I might meet a prince and become a princess in some faraway land." They hugged and giggled.

"Thank you for being my friend, Deb. It really helps to talk to you. I feel like this is a turning point in my life." She stood up and straightened her back. "I'm going to find out who I really am." She gave Debbie another quick hug. "I'd better get home. See you tomorrow. Love you."

After ruling out more serious causes, the doctor sent Aimee to an allergy specialist who determined that she had some food allergies. He placed her on a restricted diet; soon Aimee returned to being a healthy teenager. She would never return, however, to the girl she thought she was. She felt incomplete and disconnected. The same questions ran on a loop through her brain. *Where do I come from? Do I have any brothers or sisters? Why did she give me up? Is there something wrong with me? Why didn't they tell me? What else are they keeping from me?*

Although the doctors found no real problems with her health, Aimee began to believe that since her adoption had been kept from her, there must be facts that needed to be kept secret. If that was so, the facts must be bad, she reasoned. Suddenly, the carefree life she had enjoyed and her image of herself was shaken. She no longer felt in control. There was an extreme sense of loss—loss of the people she believed to be her parents, loss of birth parents she may never know. Most of all, loss of the girl she thought she was. She vowed to never trust her 'pretend' parents again. She was determined to find her real parents.

"I have to go to Bangkok on business," Martin announced one evening at dinner. "Helen, I was thinking you and Aimee might like to join me."

"That sounds wonderful. Doesn't it, Aimee?"

"I guess." Aimee mumbled. She didn't feel like talking to them, especially her mother or the person she thought was her mother, since that day at the doctor's office.

"When do we leave?" Helen asked.

"A week from Saturday. I have to meet with some officials at the bank on Monday. You girls can do some shopping. I'll join you for some sightseeing after my business is finished."

"I'll have to rearrange a committee meeting. It sounds wonderful, Martin."

"Great. So, it's settled. I'll have my secretary make all the arrangements."

"Thank you, Martin," Helen said lying in bed that night. "Maybe this trip is our chance to mend things with Aimee. She hasn't been the same since she found out."

"Don't worry, dear. You know how teenagers are. It'll be all right."

"I hope you're right. She seems to have retreated from us. She doesn't talk to me on the way to school. She goes right to her room after dinner. Maybe we should get her some kind of counseling. I'm afraid it was wrong of us not to tell her a long time ago. I hate that she found out the way she did."

"I know but that can't be helped now." Martin rolled on his side facing away from her. "Let's see how she is on the trip. If she's the same when we get back, we can look into getting her some help."

CHAPTER 13

Upon arrival in Bangkok, they were met by a representative of the bank holding a cardboard sign on which was printed 'Gordon Party'. Aimee saw the sign first and then she saw him. *He's beautiful.* She had never thought of a man as beautiful, but he was more than handsome—he was beautiful.

Kris was taller than most Thais, just shy of six feet. His skin, the creamy color of a mocha latte, and high cheekbones were the result of the union of his Austrian father and Thai mother. His almond shaped eyes were black as the onyx ring Aimee received on her sixteenth birthday. Her fingers begged to run through his straight, thick black hair combed back on the sides. *Yes, beautiful is the right word for him.*

Aimee waved at Kris. As he approached, her father came up behind her.

"I'm Martin Gordon. This is my wife, Helen, and our daughter, Aimee."

"Welcome, Mr. Gordon. I am Kris Montri from the bank," he said, bowing and extending his hand to Martin. Turning toward the women, he bowed his head slightly.

Martin's secretary had provided the family with information on protocol in Thailand so Aimee knew not to extend her hand, which was only for men, but secretly she wanted to touch this man.

"Please, follow me. We have a car waiting. The porter will get your luggage."

Kris led them outside and opened the back door of a sleek, black town car. The porter placed the luggage in the trunk. After tipping him, Kris slid into the passenger seat beside the driver. He spoke in Thai and soon they were off.

"I am to be your guide for the duration of your trip, Mr. Gordon," Kris said, turning toward the back seat. "I hope you will have a pleasurable and successful trip."

Aimee remembered thinking that he was looking directly at her as she sat between her parents. His eyes were captivating. She detected a hint of admiration when he looked at her. She averted her eyes and took in the sights outside the window. She hoped her parents didn't notice the quiver in her voice as she commented on how exciting it was to be in Bangkok.

When they entered the two-bedroom suite at the Shangri-La Hotel, Aimee stifled a squeal. It was far more luxurious than the hotel where they had stayed in Rome. Two walls of the corner suite had large windows that provided an impressive, uninterrupted view of the Chao Phraya River with its double-decker tour boats. There was a basket of fruit on a marble-topped teak coffee table and a large floral arrangement of orchids and hibiscus on a narrow teak table behind the gold silk upholstered sofa. Through an archway was a rectangular dining table flanked by teak chairs upholstered to match the sofa. A chandelier hanging from a circular alcove ceiling cast a soft glow.

"I'm sure you would like to get some rest after your long trip," Kris said. "You are all invited this evening to dinner at the home of our bank president, Mr. Anon. Here is your itinerary for the next two days," he said, handing Martin a folder. "Of course, Mr. Gordon, you may rearrange it to your pleasure. I will pick you up at six o'clock which is three hours from now. Ladies, you will want to wear sandals for dinner as you will be required to remove them at the door. Mr. Gordon, you may leave your socks on after removing your shoes. Do you have any questions?"

"No," Martin said. "Thank you very much, Kris. We appreciate your assistance."

Kris extended his hand to Martin and made a slight bow toward the ladies. For a moment, he held his gaze on Aimee. She felt the warmth rise in her cheeks.

Dressing for dinner in the marble-floored bathroom, Aimee was sorry that protocol required her to wear the blue and yellow paisley print dress with its high, scoop neck, puffed sleeves, and flared skirt that covered her knees. It made her look young and that wasn't how she wanted Kris Montri to think of her.

CHAPTER 14

Aimee watched Kris stride across the glistening marble and chandelier-lit lobby toward them. He was even more handsome in his midnight blue, tailored suit that followed all the lines of his lean, muscular body. He made a slight bow to the women and extended his hand to Aimee's father.

"Ready to go?" he asked, leading them outside to their black town car. He slid in beside the driver and turned toward them in the back seat.

"You will be joined this evening by Mr. Anon's family and Mr. Huron, who is on the board of the bank and owns one of the largest silk-manufacturing businesses in Bangkok," Kris said. "As is our custom, there will be no business discussed during the meal. We like to only enjoy our friends and our food, business comes later," he said.

"That's wonderful, Kris," Helen said. "I think I'll adopt Thai rules when we get home, Martin."

"Yes, dear," Martin said, cocking his head toward her and looking over his rimless glasses.

As they left the skyscrapers of the city, Aimee was surprised to see homes that could have been in Savannah. The architecture had a colonial feel with arches and pillars. Lush tropical palms, ferns, and pink and fuchsia flowering plants protected the houses from full view.

Turning into a winding drive, Aimee could just make out the top of a house with an aqua tile roof. Chartreuse ferns and glossy dark green hibiscus crowned in red flowers parted to reveal a light yellow house with white pillars along the front porch. A second level was set back from the porch roof. Its arched windows were in contrast with large rectangular picture windows flanking the teak double doors of the main entrance.

Stepping onto the porch, Aimee noticed a pair of men's shoes neatly placed on a large bamboo rug. Kris quickly slipped out of his shoes and the Gordons followed suit. The double doors opened, and Kris greeted a servant dressed in loose, white cotton trousers and a long-sleeved shirt that fell to his knees.

The entrance hall was paneled in teak. On the two side walls sat narrow, ornately carved teak tables topped with matching bronze Thai Princess Statues. Candles flickered in hammered brass cylinders.

The servant escorted them into the living room. A picture window, framed by five-foot palm plants in large celadon ceramic vases, flooded the room with light, in stark contrast to the dark entryway. Aimee was not surprised to see two red silk brocade sofas flanked by carved teak chairs upholstered in red and gold striped silk. Her protocol book said that these colors signified happiness and luck to the Thai people. She loved the gold throw pillows embossed with silver elephants.

Their hosts, Mr. Anon and his wife, entered the room.

"Mr. and Mrs. Gordon and Miss Gordon, welcome to my home. This is my wife, Sunee, and our friend, Mano Huron. Good to see you Kris."

The men shook hands and the women made slight bows toward each other.

"I hope you had a comfortable trip from the States and found your accommodations to be to your liking," Mr. Anon said.

"Yes," Martin said. "And we are so honored to be in your lovely home."

"We are honored you could join us. Shall we go into the dining room?" Mr. Anon said, motioning them toward an archway across from the picture window.

The dining room table was made of teak with intricately carved legs matched by the carving on the backs of the yellow silk upholstered chairs. The walls were hung with rectangular silk panels embroidered with colorful flowers and birds. A crystal chandelier cast a mellow light on the table set with dark bamboo oval mats topped with white ceramic plates edged in graceful ferns and tiny red flowers. The crystal glasses and red napkins placed like fans on the plates completed the setting. It was both elegant and casual.

Two servants pulled out the chairs. Mr. Anon was seated at one end of the table with Martin on his left and Mr. Huron on his right. Mrs. Anon was seated at the other end with Helen on her left and Aimee on her right. Aimee was pleased when Kris seated himself beside her. Just as Aimee noticed the empty seat across from Kris, a lovely young woman who looked to be Aimee's age came bounding into the room. The servant quickly pulled out the chair for her.

"This is my daughter, Chantana," Mr. Anon said, his tone revealing his displeasure at her late arrival. "This is Mr. and Mrs. Gordon and their daughter, Aimee."

"I'm so sorry. I got out of class late. It's wonderful to meet all of you," she said, flipping her dark hair over her shoulder with her hand. "Nice to see you again, Kris."

Aimee felt a stab of jealousy when she detected something flash between them.

"It smells wonderful," Aimee said as the servant delivered red bowls of soup. "I've had Thai food in Los Angeles but I'm sure it's nothing like this."

"It is a traditional Thai soup called Tom Kha Gai," Sunee Anon said. "It is made of mushrooms, pieces of chicken and lots of coconut milk. It is a bit sour because of the lemongrass, kaffir lime leaves, and cilantro. I hope you like it."

"We use cilantro in our Mexican food," Aimee offered.

"This is delicious," Helen Gordon said, delicately dipping her spoon into the thick soup, lifting it to her lips and sipping slowly.

Noticing the puzzled look on Aimee's face when she saw only a fork and spoon, Kris leaned close to her ear.

"We use the fork in our left hand to scoop the food into the spoon. We don't use knives and we rarely use chopsticks, except for rice."

"Thank you," Aimee whispered.

"Are you still in school, Aimee?" Chantana asked.

"Yes, I'll graduate from high school in June. I'm on spring break."

"I'm a freshman in college. I really like it but it's challenging. I'm majoring in fashion."

"I love your dress. Did you design it?" Aimee asked, admiring the dark blue silk sheath covered in white hibiscus flowers, with cap sleeves and a mandarin collar. She really hated how childish she must look in her paisley dress.

"No, but it's the type of dress I want to design; modern, yet with some of the traditional style of our country. Kris, I hope you plan to take Aimee and her mother shopping tomorrow. We have so many lovely shops."

"Yes, that is on our agenda," Kris said, sounding a bit annoyed.

Aimee felt tension between them.

As the servants delivered one intriguing dish after another, the women talked about shopping and the most important temples to visit. At the other end of the table, the men were talking about golf and soccer. *Just like home,* Aimee thought. She couldn't help but notice that Mr. Huron directed his gaze toward her frequently. *He's not bad looking. He has to be the same age as my father.* Aimee leaned over to Kris. "Does Mr. Huron have a wife?" she whispered.

"Yes, but she usually doesn't attend social functions with him," Kris said, and quickly changed the subject. "So, how do you like Thai food?"

"It's good. Much better than what I ate in California."

"Here comes the dessert. It's my favorite. It's our version of an ice cream sandwich—coconut ice cream in a bun with sweet sticky rice on the bottom, peanuts and preserved palm fruit."

After dinner, their hosts invited them out to the terrace, heavy with the scent of jasmine. Mrs. Anon led the women to one side of the garden.

"I want to show you our rare Parrot flower," she said, lifting an orchid whose crimson curved base and pale pink body fell into purple-tipped petals forming a parrot shape.

"Why, it does look just like a parrot," Helen exclaimed.

Aimee particularly liked the koi pond surrounded by smooth rocks pointing the way to a large stone Buddha who seemed to be surveying the schools of gold and orange carp happily swimming below floating pads topped by pink and white lilies. The soft lights and the full moon created a magical, peaceful retreat.

Glancing across the garden at Kris, Aimee smiled and briefly forgot about her jealousy over Chantana. He gave her a reassuring smile and started toward her. Before he could reach her, Mr. Huron approached and grabbed his arm. Turning their backs to the garden, he bent his head toward Kris. Kris nodded slightly, glanced over his shoulder at Aimee and back to Huron.

I wonder what that's about? Once again, she felt uncomfortable.

Aimee couldn't know that their conversation would change the course of her life dramatically.

Kris turned aside and made his way across the garden to Aimee.

"Mr. Huron was just suggesting some places you and your mother might like to visit. I'd better get you back to the hotel. We have a big day tomorrow."

CHAPTER 15

Early the next morning as Aimee dressed for their shopping trip, she wondered if Kris and Chantana had been a couple. Although they were cordial with each other, it reminded her of the way her friends acted when they were around their ex-boyfriends. She hoped Kris had no interest in Chantana. She hoped he had an interest in her. She would soon find out.

"Sorry to get you up so early," Kris said, escorting Aimee and her mother, Helen, to their black town car, "but I'm taking you to the Damnoen Saduak Floating Market. It's like nothing you've ever seen."

"Oh, I've read about it," Helen exclaimed. "I think it was in one of the James Bond movies."

"You're right, Mrs. Gordon. If you hadn't heard of it before, that movie certainly made it famous."

Upon arrival, Kris escorted them to the dock along the canal. It was filled with long, highly polished, wooden canoes piloted by old ladies wearing flat straw hats. The space between the boats was so narrow that Aimee couldn't see how they could move at all but move they did. Fruits and vegetables of every color and variety filled the boats. The smell of fish and river water mingled with the scent of curry-laden Thai noodle soup. The shouts of the boat ladies hawking their wares and negotiating with the shoppers on the dock created a cacophony that, strangely, was not unpleasant to the ear. The women expertly maneuvered their boats with long paddles; making room when one needed to move close to their customer on the dock. There seemed to be a rhythm to it all. It created a floating feast for all the senses. Aimee loved it. She felt more alive in this strange land than she had ever felt back home, especially now.

"Oh, Kris," she exclaimed, her eyes bright with excitement. "I love it. It's like something out of a movie."

"A James Bond movie," her mother laughed. Aimee rolled her eyes.

"I want to take some pictures," Aimee said, pulling her camera out of her backpack and handing it to Kris. "Kris, please take a picture of my mother and me, then she can take our picture."

"Smile, that's nice."

"Now you two," Helen said, reaching out to Kris for the camera.

"Move closer to Aimee, Kris," Helen said. "That's it. Smile. Good."

Aimee knew he couldn't put his arm around her as a boy in the States would have, but she felt he wanted to. It made her stomach flutter. She didn't notice that Kris turned his head to the right away from her just as the camera flashed.

"If you ladies are ready, our next stop is the famous Chatuchak Weekend Market. That's where you'll find the dresses Chantana told you about."

Chatuchak Weekend Market was the largest open-air market Aimee had ever seen. The rows of stalls displayed everything from clothing to antiques to plants to pets. Three-sided bins held neatly folded shirts in every color of the rainbow. Hats of bamboo, straw and cloth were stacked three feet high. Silk scarves and wraps were draped over clotheslines next to fine leather shoulder bags, handbags, and printed backpacks. A light breeze failed to dispel the stifling heat created by the sun and the press of humanity in the narrow walkways between the stalls. If the floating market had been a satisfying feast, the open market was more like a crowded buffet with everyone jostling each other to fill their plates with more than they would ever be able to eat.

Kris herded them through the shoppers into a stall that was wider and deeper than the rest. Aimee was grateful for the large rotating fan at the entrance. Kris greeted a man he introduced as the owner who bowed to the women.

"Mr. Sura welcomes you. If you wish to try on any of the clothes, there are two dressing rooms at the back behind those curtains," Kris gestured. "Take your time."

Aimee sorted through the Thai silk dresses on a circular rack. Suddenly she was aware that Kris was standing behind her so close she could feel his breath on her neck. He leaned down as though he was commenting on a particular garment, pressing his hand lightly on the small of her back.

"You know, Aimee, it's not proper for me to hold your hand or kiss you in public," he whispered, "but I want you to know that is what I would like to do."

Aimee turned and looked up at him. She felt her cheeks flush.

"I would like that too."

He moved away quickly when Helen approached carrying several dresses.

"Try these, Aimee. I think they would look wonderful on you. My, dear, are you too warm? Your face is flushed."

"No, Mother, I'm fine. Let me try them on." She glanced at Kris and felt the warmth creeping up her neck. *He's so sexy and he wants to kiss me!*

When Kris dropped them off after their day of shopping, Martin was back from his meetings.

"I was telling the ladies that I would be happy to take you all to see some temples tomorrow."

"That's very kind of you. However, I won't be able to come" Martin said. "I have my last meeting at the bank tomorrow. I had hoped I could join you girls, but it's taking longer than I expected. I'm sorry."

"That's all right, dear," Helen said. "Kris is taking quite good care of us." She turned to Kris. "What time should we be ready?"

"We will leave early as it will be cooler and there will be fewer people. I will pick you up at seven thirty. The temples are sacred places so you must dress appropriately, nothing short or revealing."

"We read about that in our protocol manual. We'll be ready and thank you so much, Kris, for the lovely day," Helen said.

Kris was an excellent tour guide. He seemed to take great pride in sharing the history of his country.

"The word "*Wat*" means temple," Kris explained. "The monks live in the temple complexes. They rise at four in the morning for their prayers and duties. Then you will see them in their saffron-colored robes emerge to collect food and necessities from the people on the street."

The first temple they visited was Wat Traimit, home of the famed Golden Buddha. They stared in awe at the ten-foot, solid-gold statue weighing some 5.5 tons.

"In the past, after they were crafted in gold, they were covered in stucco and plaster to hide them from invading armies. This Buddha was discovered by accident when it was dropped in a move revealing the gold statue under the plaster," Kris said. "Next, we will visit Wat Pho, the oldest and largest of our temples, to see the reclining Buddha. It is forty-six meters long."

"I can't imagine anything more impressive than this golden Buddha," Helen said, "but forty-six meters of Buddha may do it."

Aimee loved the history Kris shared and marveled at his knowledge. She didn't want to think about leaving Bangkok and this exciting man.

At their last stop, Wat Benchamabophit, an impressive temple built out of slabs of marble imported from Italy, a strange thing happened. A disheveled young woman approached them shouting something in Thai at Kris. He headed toward her, stopping her before she reached Helen and Aimee. He grasped her arm and turned her away from them. He bent his head down and spoke to her in Thai. Then he pressed something in her hand. She stumbled away toward the temple entrance.

"Just a beggar," Kris said, returning to Aimee and Helen. "They like to hang around the temples and get money from the tourists. I'm sorry about that."

That's strange, Aimee thought, *I didn't understand what she was saying, but I'm sure she called him by name.*

Since they were returning to the States the next morning, Mr. and Mrs. Anon invited the Gordon family to dinner at an elegant Thai restaurant that evening. Once again, Mr. Huron joined them without his wife. Once again, his admiring glances made Aimee uneasy.

The men discussed golf and Helen told Mrs. Anon about their visit to the temples. Aimee looked across the table at Kris. She didn't want to go home. She wondered if she would get that kiss before they left.

CHAPTER 16

Now, as Aimee sat on the bed in the tiny house in Los Angeles waiting for Kris, she smiled. She had gotten that kiss in the darkened hallway outside the ladies room in that elegant Thai restaurant. That kiss and the way Kris held her pressed against him was all she dreamt about when she got home. He took her email address and promised he would write. Three days after she returned from Bangkok, she was thrilled to read:

Aimee, you only left me a few days ago but it seems like months. I can't get you out of my mind. Our kiss that last night left me wanting more. You are not like any other woman I know. Not only are you beautiful but you are sweet and kind. I hope you will answer me soon and tell me if you feel as I do. I am so happy you came to Bangkok and we met. Fan hwan (that is Thai for sweet dreams) Kris

Aimee remembered feeling so happy when he called her a woman. She couldn't wait to tell Debbie.

Kris, I was so happy to hear from you. Yes, I miss you too. Being in Bangkok seems like a dream now. It's been difficult since I came home. I wish you were here. I think of you all the time. Will we ever see each other again? Sweet Dreams, Aimee

Dearest Aimee, You say it has been difficult. What's difficult? Tell me about it. Maybe I can help you. I don't like to hear that you are unhappy. Please tell me what is making you so unhappy. Fan hwan, Kris

Dear Kris, My parents brought me with them to Bangkok because I was angry with them over what happened. They thought the trip would help. Right before we came to Bangkok, I found out, by accident, that I am adopted! They kept this big secret from me. My entire life has been a lie. I always wondered why I don't look like anyone in my family. Now, I wonder if everyone in the family knew but me! I keep thinking there might be worse things about me they're not telling me. I don't feel I can trust anything they say. I feel like such an outsider. I don't know what to do. Aimee

Darling Aimee, I'm so sorry to hear this. I can understand why that would be very upsetting. I know what you mean about feeling like an outsider. As you may have guessed, I am of mixed race. My father is Austrian and my mother is Thai. When I was little, I was bullied. I believe you have that in America also. My father left us when I was ten. I, too, was angry. I thought he left because of me. When I got older, my mother told me why he left and that it had nothing to do with me. It isn't right that your parents didn't tell you that you are adopted. Do you know anything about your real father and mother? I wish I could hold and kiss you right now. Fan hwan, Kris

Dear Kris, Thank you for telling me about your father. I wish I knew about my real father and mother. Why did they give me up? Helen and Martin have been good to me. I haven't wanted for anything material, but they are older than my friends' parents. Sometimes, I feel like they don't understand me. I wonder how old my real parents are and where they live. I might have passed my real mother on the street! I can't go back to who I was, but I don't know how to figure out who I am. I think I need to find out who they are and where they are. Thank you for caring about me. Sleep tight, Aimee

When a few days went by and she didn't hear from him, she worried she might have said too much, and he wouldn't want to be with her anymore. After all, they were thousands of miles away from each other, and why would he want her when he could have his pick among the exotic Thai women?

Dearest, I'm so sorry I haven't written. I was away on business. It hurts me that you are so sad. I've been thinking about how we can be together. When do you finish school? You haven't told your parents about our emails, have you? I'm afraid they might try to keep us apart. I will never lie to you. We are meant to be together. I'm working on a plan. Love Kris.

It was the first time he said he loved her. It was just like one of her romance novels. She raced over to Debbie's house.

"I wonder what he means about having a plan," Debbie said. "Do you think he's going to come and see you?"

"I don't know. That would be wonderful. You could meet him." Aimee lay across Debbie's bed. "He's not like any boy I've ever known. He's a real man."

"It's all very romantic. I wish his face wasn't turned away in the picture you have of him, but I can kinda tell that he's good looking."

"I know. I wish Mother had noticed and taken another one. He looks like a movie star and he's so sexy."

They dissolved into giggles.

Dear Kris, I've decided I don't want to go to college after I graduate. I've always wanted to travel. It was such a magical time with you in Thailand. I'm going to tell Father and Mother I want to get a job with the airlines. I think I'd make a very good flight attendant. They won't be happy about me not going to college, but I'll be eighteen soon and they won't be able to stop me. What do you think? xoxoxo Aimee

Dear Aimee, I think you would be a very good flight attendant. You're certainly pretty enough and you're smart. I know some people at Thai Airways. I could talk to them about getting you an interview. It would be so wonderful to have you with me in Thailand. We could travel together. You know I'm a very good tour guide. Love, Kris

Dearest Kris, I'm excited to think about being with you. I graduate next week. I need to get that job with Thai Airways to have the money to leave home. I haven't told my parents yet. They're not going to be happy. I've been trying to find any documents in the house that would help me find out who my real mother is but nothing yet. Helen told me it was a closed adoption. Ever since I found out I'm not their child, I can't think of them as my parents. I'm so miserable. Thinking about you is what keeps me going. Love, Aimee

Dearest, It hurts me to hear how unhappy you are. We need to be together. I love you. I want to take care of you. Darling, I want to marry you. You and I

will make our own family. Come to Thailand after you graduate and marry me.
I will help you get a job with Thai Airways after you get here. I have connections.
Please say yes. Love Kris

Aimee tossed and turned that night. *He loves me. He'll take care of me.*
I felt so at home in Thailand. I can be me; not the adopted child whose parents
didn't want her. I'll travel; we'll travel. She hugged her pillow. She would tell
Debbie tomorrow.

"I'm going over to Debbie's," she shouted to Helen.

"You just got home from school. I have a committee meeting tonight so
we're having dinner at five thirty."

"I'll be back in time. We just need to talk about what we're wearing
for graduation."

When Debbie opened her door, Aimee grabbed her arm and pushed
her toward her bedroom.

"What's going on?" Debbie asked, stumbling down the hall.

Aimee shut the door. "Kris asked me to marry him!" she said
breathlessly.

"What? What do you mean? Is he coming here?"

"No, he wants me to come to Thailand. He'll help me get a job with
Thai Airways and we'll get married. Isn't it exciting? I'll have my dream job
and my dream man."

"What will your parents say? You'll be leaving your home and moving
to a strange country with someone you hardly know. Besides, I thought we
were going to travel together."

"Be honest, Deb, you know you're going to go to college like your parents want you to and then where will I be? You'll be off doing your thing and
soon have a boyfriend yourself. I can't stay here and be the person my parents
want me to be. Kris loves me; he gets me. I can be myself with him. If you read
his emails, you'd see how sweet and caring he is." Aimee took Debbie's hands

in hers. "I can't go on pretending I'm Helen and Martin's daughter anymore. I don't have any family anymore. I'm sure the Gordon family has known all along that I was adopted. How can I trust any of them anymore? You say I hardly know him, but I know him better than I know them."

"I can't imagine what you're feeling. I'm worried, but if this is really what you want, I'm happy for you. Please promise me you'll take enough money with you to come home if it doesn't work out. I'll miss you so much." Debbie grabbed her and hugged her tightly.

"I'll miss you too but you can come and visit me." Aimee released herself from Debbie's arms and stepped back. "I know I'm getting a graduation gift of a thousand dollars from my parents and probably a little more from other family members. I promise I'll keep it safe and I'll come straight back if I'm not happy."

"When will you leave?"

"I don't know yet. Kris and I will have to make our plans."

Dearest Aimee, I have decided that I should come to Los Angeles and bring you back to Bangkok with me. I don't want you to have to fly alone. Don't tell your parents or they might try to stop us. We can let them know our plans as soon as we get to Bangkok. I will make all of the arrangements and pay for your ticket. When is the best time for me to come? It should probably be a weekday when your parents aren't home. I will come to the house and pick you up. We can leave for Bangkok the next day. Can you tell them you are staying with a friend that night? Darling, I can't wait to be with you. Please advise the best date. Love Kris

Aimee checked her mother's calendar and chose the Monday after graduation when her father would be at work and her mother was hosting a women's luncheon at the country club. As expected, they had given her the graduation money at the restaurant where they celebrated with Helen's sister and her husband, Martin's brother and his wife, and her cousins. She was happy to receive their gifts of money as well, but she couldn't help noticing how kind they were being. She knew it must be about the whole adoption thing.

When they arrived home from the party, Martin poured champagne for the three of them and toasted her accomplishment. Aimee sat down in the chair across from them and took a deep breath.

"I need to tell you about what I want to do now that I've graduated."

"What do you mean? I thought you wanted to take some time off this summer before you start college," Martin said.

"I'm not going to college." She straightened up in the chair and set her shoulders. "You know how I've always wanted to travel. I want to get a job with the airlines."

"What do you mean you're not going to college?" Helen's voice rose. "What on earth brought this on? You've always planned to go to college."

"No, you've always planned for me to go to college, Mother. But I've changed my mind. A lot of things have changed since I found out I'm adopted!"

"What has that got to do with anything?" Helen plunked her champagne glass down hard on the coffee table. "Why do you want to ruin your future; a wonderful future we have planned for you. You're our daughter and always have been. Just because I didn't give birth to you doesn't mean you're not mine." She pulled a tissue out of the pocket of her dress and patted at the tears forming.

"Aimee, you're upsetting your mother. I know you've been angry that we didn't tell you that you were adopted, but that's no reason to throw away all the plans we've made for you. Let's talk about this tomorrow. I'm sure we can figure something out that will make everyone happy," Martin said, patting Helen's hand. "It's been a long day. Let's all sleep on it."

Aimee rose and looked down at Helen. "I'm sorry, Mother. I didn't mean to hurt you. Father's right. I've got plenty of time to figure out what's right for me. I'm tired. Let's go to bed."

When Aimee got to her room, she sent an email to Kris telling him what had happened with her parents and gave him the date he could come to get her. She didn't bring up college again and her parents seemed happy to ignore her change of mind.

The excitement of preparing for Kris's arrival and his continued reassurance of his love bolstered Aimee until she received his call and left her house and her parents. Carrying her Louis Vuitton bag and her Coach Crossbody bag bouncing on her hip, she flew down the steps into his waiting arms. He gave her a hug and looked up at her house.

"Are you sure no one saw you leave?"

"No, everyone's gone. I'm so happy to see you."

He quickly opened the door of the rental car and took her bag as she jumped in. He rounded the car to the driver's side, slung her bag in the back seat, opened his door and slid in. Leaning across the console, he placed his hand on her jean-clad thigh and kissed her deeply. She felt her heart flutter when the tip of his tongue darted into her mouth.

"I can't believe I finally have you with me again," he said. "You're even prettier than I remembered. Do you have your passport? Do you think your parents suspect anything?"

"No. The only person who knows about us is my girlfriend Debbie and she won't tell. I left my parents a note saying I was spending the night at her house. She'll cover for me. I have my passport," she said, touching it inside her purse. "I've missed you so much." She placed her hand on top of his. "Did you really mean all of those things you said in your emails?"

"I told you that night in the restaurant that we were meant to be together. I love you. I'll take good care of you. You believe me, don't you?"

"Oh, yes. I've never felt like this before. I love you too."

"What did you tell your friend about us? Are you sure she won't tell anyone?"

"Debbie is my best friend. I told her all about how we met and about how, after we're married, you're going to help me get a job with the airlines. She thinks it's all very romantic. In fact," Aimee laughed, "she can't wait to come and visit us."

Now, lying on the bed in this little house, Aimee suddenly felt homesick. She wished she could call her parents, but she knew they would try to stop her. Besides, she reminded herself, they weren't her real parents. She'd email them when she got to Bangkok.

When she heard the door open, she jumped off the bed to greet Kris.

"Here's the pizza. Did you get some rest?"

"Not much. I was remembering our first meeting and our time in Bangkok," she said, reaching up, circling her arms around his neck and kissing him. "You must show me all your favorite places. I can't wait to meet your family and friends."

He gave her a quick hug and laid the box on the small table.

"Here, have some pizza and I brought you a cola."

CHAPTER 17

MARGO

M argo's heart leapt when she opened the company email and saw Rick's name.

We are saddened to report the passing of Carol Cathcart, wife of Senior Vice President, Operations, Richard Cathcart. Carol lost her battle with cancer on Friday, July 7, 1998. A memorial service will be held at Rose Hills Mortuary in Whittier CA, on Friday, July 14, at 2:00 p.m. In lieu of flowers, the family has requested that donations be made in Carol's name to the American Cancer Society. Our heartfelt sympathy goes out to Rick and Carol's family.

For the first two years after Rick moved to Seattle, he would remember Margo with a card on holidays and her birthday. She had never reciprocated. It was too hard to be reminded of their time together and their baby she had given up. Now she felt a real sorrow for his loss. She knew he and Carol had never had children. *What would he say if he knew he had a daughter and that she was missing? Should she go to the memorial? Could she go to the memorial?*

When Margo arrived home from work, she was still pondering what to do when the phone rang.

"Kitt? It's me." The familiar voice was weak and filled with sadness. "I guess you heard about Carol."

Margo felt the tears well up when she heard his pet name for her.

"Yes. I'm so sorry, Rick. I read the email at work last night. How long had she been ill?"

"Two years. I can't believe she's gone. I tried to be a better husband in the end. I wasn't a very good one as you know but I tried to be in the end."

Margo felt a pang of guilt. She had helped him be a bad husband. She searched for the right thing to say. "I'm sure you did all you could. There's nothing anyone can say right now that will help, but I'm sure you did your best." Her heart ached for him. She really had loved him; maybe she still did.

"Thank you, Kitt. I hope you can come to the memorial. It'll be good to see you." His voice was husky. "Are you doing okay?"

"Yes, I'm fine," Margo said, quickly composing herself. "I'll try to come. Get some rest and take care of yourself." Her hands were shaking as she hung up the phone. *What would it be like to see him again?*

The phone rang again jolting her out of her thoughts.

"Margo, it's Sam. Sam Carpenter."

"Hello, Sam," she said, clearing her voice. "Do you have news about Aimee?"

"Yes, I'm sorry to say we just got a report from Customs that she departed LAX this morning on a flight to Bangkok. We didn't get the information in time to send someone to talk to her. Immigration didn't see her passport on our watch list until their shift changed. Somebody out there is going to be in a lot of trouble."

"Do you know if she was travelling with anyone?"

"Yes, we believe she was with the passenger who had the seat beside her. A guy named Kris Montri. According to her father, he is employed by the bank and was their guide on their trip to Bangkok a couple of months ago. Her mother said Aimee was quite taken with him. We're searching Aimee's email correspondence, but I think we're going to find she went of her own free will."

"Does that mean she's not involved in any sex trafficking operation?" Margo asked hopefully. *Maybe there would be some good news today.*

"Well, I wish I could say that, but we still don't know how or why this Kris guy got her to go back with him to Thailand without her parents' knowledge. Are you okay, Margo? Your voice sounds different."

"I'm okay. The wife of a friend of mine just died so I was on the phone with him before you called." Margo wondered what Sam would think if he knew the "friend" was Aimee's father.

"I'm sorry," Sam said. After a long pause, he continued. "If you're not busy this weekend, how would you like to split a pizza with me?"

Margo's heart leapt for the second time in an hour; then her brow furrowed. *Was he asking her out or did he still think she was involved in Aimee's disappearance?*

Before she could answer, Sam said, "There's no obligation. I just thought it sounds like you're having a rough time what with Aimee missing and your friend's wife dying. It's okay if you'd rather not."

"No, no, I'd like that. I'm off work Saturday."

"Great. I'll pick you up at 7:00 p.m."

"I'd rather meet you." Once again, Margo realized she was embarrassed about where she lived. "Where do you want to go?"

"How about California Pizza Kitchen in Santa Monica?

"Sounds good. See you there."

CHAPTER 18

Although Rick didn't know it, it was Margurite who attended the memorial for his wife. It was Margo's way of protecting herself from the old feelings or making a fool of herself or, worse yet, telling him her secret. Margurite knew how to be confident and in control. She chose a deep purple silk dress that hugged her curves in a tasteful way. Her graceful neck was draped in a two-strand pearl necklace. She was always surprised how powerful she felt when Margurite took over. Scanning the room, she made out Rick's profile surrounded by top executives from the company. Age had been good to him. He was maybe even more handsome. She felt a wave of love and compassion well up. Deciding to wait to approach him until after the service, Margo moved toward a group of her co-workers.

"Hi, Margo," Tom said, welcoming her into the group. "Wow, you look nice. Do you know Mr. Cathcart? He's such a good guy. I worked with him in Denver for a while. It sure is too bad. I don't think they had any children. It was just the two of them. She was really nice too."

"I worked for him at the airport here in Los Angeles before he got promoted to Seattle," Margo replied. "He was a really good manager. We hated to see him leave, but we were happy for him." She pushed away the memory of their last night together.

Sitting in one of the back rows, she found it difficult to watch the video of Rick and Carol's life together. She noticed the back of Rick's head slumped forward and then popped back up as the video moved from their college days to their marriage to their vacations around the world. The president of the airline spoke about the way Carol supported Rick in his career and what a wonderful representative she was for the company. Carol's brother spoke about their childhood and the courage she showed in her battle with cancer. His acknowledgement of what a fine husband Rick had been and how he was by Carol's side through that battle somehow tempered the guilt Margo was feeling.

When they moved into the adjoining room where a buffet was laid out, Margo took an iced tea from the table and searched for a safe corner where Rick could approach her without their conversation being overheard.

Rick strode toward her and gave her a quick, side hug. "Kitt, thanks for coming. You look wonderful."

"It was a lovely service. How are you holding up?" Margo asked, fully aware of the attraction he still held for her and the curious glances of her co-workers in the room.

"I'm doing okay. We had a small service in Seattle on Tuesday, so it was a little easier today. There were so many people here in Los Angeles who wanted to come and couldn't get away so the company asked if they could put something together here. It's nice to see so many old friends, especially you," Rick said, touching her elbow lightly. "It's been a long time. I've missed you," he added, his voice suddenly intimate. "Do you think we could get together to catch up before I go back to Seattle?" She saw the hope in his eyes.

Don't do it, Margurite's voice in her head cautioned.

"How long will you be here?" Margo heard herself asking.

"I'm planning to fly back Sunday night. Are you available tomorrow? We could have brunch at our favorite place in Santa Monica. Is it still around?"

"No, I don't think so. Actually, I have plans tomorrow," Margurite responded for her.

"How about Sunday?" Rick persisted. "I'm staying at the Ritz Carlton in Marina Del Rey. They have a world class Sunday brunch. I'll make a reservation for eleven thirty. How's that? It'll be great to catch up."

"Okay, that'll be nice. See you Sunday. It was a lovely service."

"I guess I didn't even ask. Are you married?"

"No," Margurite answered brightly for her. "I've had too much fun exploring the world."

Margo couldn't wait to get out of there. She thought about turning around and telling him she had forgotten she had to work on Sunday, but truthfully, she wanted to see him without all of these people around. She was surprised to find the tears welling up as she hailed a taxi. She was glad she decided not to drive her old beat-up car. She needed to get it washed and cleaned out before she met Sam.

Getting ready to meet Sam, she realized she wanted to look like Margurite, but behave like Margo. Never before had her duality been so apparent to her. For such a long time, Margo the bag lady was who she felt she really was; it was all she deserved to be. Now, she was confused. She was confident and flirtatious when she put Margurite in charge. But that's not who she wanted to be with Sam. She wanted to be the old Margo, the one Rick remembered. She knew she couldn't be that girl again either. Too much had happened to that girl. In the end, she opted for a toned-down version of Margurite, more stylish than the old Margo, but not as perfect as Margurite. Not Rick's Margo but maybe Sam's Margo.

When she arrived at the restaurant, Sam was waiting outside looking even more handsome in tight, dark jeans and a black chino military jacket. She knew by the look on his face she had made the right choice by wearing Margurite's black jumpsuit topped with a daffodil yellow bomber jacket.

"Hi, you look great!" he said, opening the door for her. "I'm glad you could make it."

Margo felt the warmth on her cheeks. It had been a long time since she felt admired.

After they ordered their pizza, Sam leaned across the table and clasped her hand in both of his. She felt an electric shock.

"How are you doing?" he asked, his eyes fixed on hers.

"I'm okay," she said, quickly sliding her hands from his clasp. *Did he feel it too?* "Of course, I think about Aimee all the time. I feel so helpless. I know you and your people are doing all you can, but now that she's left the country, do you even have any more to do with the case?"

Sam leaned back in his chair. "Not officially, but I'm continuing to follow any leads. I can tell you I've just received copies of the emails between Aimee and this Kris guy. It appears she's in love with him and planned to run away with him. I don't know if he's really in love with her. He was certainly saying all the right things, but that's what bothers me. Most young men in love don't know how to say the right things." Sam didn't tell her that Kris's emails smacked of a predator grooming his prey.

"Anyway, we're waiting on background information on him. Aimee's father wanted to get in touch with Mr. Anon from the bank. We asked him to hold off so Montri won't be tipped off that we're tracking him. We don't have enough information for the FBI to get involved at this point, especially since, by all appearances, she went of her own free will. I know it's difficult and I'm sorry that's all I have to tell you right now."

"Thank you, Sam. I know you're doing all you can. I just can't stop thinking about what she might be going through. Maybe if they really are in love, he won't hurt her," she said hopefully.

During dinner, they made small talk and Margo began to relax.

"Shall we take a walk on the pier?" Sam asked.

"That would be nice. It's such a beautiful evening." She was surprised and pleased when he took her hand as they strolled past other couples on the Santa Monica pier. At one point, Sam stopped and they peered down at the waves gently lapping against the pylons. The full moon cast a path of shimmering light across the water to their spot. It seemed only natural when he leaned down and kissed her. It was a perfect kiss, a perfect night, a perfect date. She didn't want it to end. The thought of her brunch tomorrow with Rick and whether she should tell him about Aimee made her pull away from Sam. *Is my baby still alive? What is she going through?* She shivered.

"What's the matter? I thought you wanted…"

She put her hand to his lips. "It's not you, Sam. I did want you to kiss me and it was very nice, but I thought of what might be happening to Aimee right now."

He pulled her into his arms. "Even though it's no longer my case, I promise you I'll do everything I can to help find her."

CHAPTER 19

When Margo walked into the lobby of the Ritz Carlton, she felt nervous and excited all at once. Her date with Sam brought back memories of her time with Rick. When he rose from a chair in the lobby and came towards her, it could have been a time eighteen years ago; the only sign that he had aged was the silver at his temples. She took a deep breath to steady herself.

"It's so good to see you, Kitt," he said, giving her a brief hug. "I'm anxious to catch up on your life."

He took her arm and linked it through his, guiding her towards the restaurant. It was familiar and comfortable. She didn't like the feeling. They passed the buffet table laden with everything from lobster and shrimp to colorful salads to a variety of pastries. A chef stood at the end of the table preparing omelets made to order. She was glad when they were seated at a corner table for two by an open window. If she decided to tell him about Aimee, at least the whole restaurant wouldn't hear her secret. Since it was Sunday, the harbor was busy with boats of every variety. The seagulls sat on posts or strutted along the walk hoping for a benefactor on this bright, sunny day. The salty breeze calmed her.

"It was a lovely memorial." She leaned toward him, searching his face. "How are you doing, Rick?"

"I'm okay. I guess it really hasn't sunk in yet. You know, you sit by them day after day and hope for a miracle until you begin to hope for relief for them and you." Rick sighed. He leaned forward and fixed those familiar blue eyes on hers. "It's so good to see you. I guess I already said that but it's true. I've thought of you often and wondered how you were doing."

Margo was relieved when the waiter interrupted to take their order. All the while she was looking at the menu, Margo wondered if she should tell Rick about Aimee. She didn't even know how she would begin.

As they ate, they chatted about the company and people they knew in common, being careful not to talk about the past. Rick shared with her that his next promotion was going to bring him back to Los Angeles. When she heard that, she noticed a slight cramping in her stomach. She wondered what that might mean for her, for them.

"So, you never married? I'm sure you've had plenty of chances. You're such a great gal. Oh, sorry, you probably have a boyfriend."

"No one serious," Margo said as she thought about Sam's kiss on the pier.

He gazed out the window and watched a young mother holding her son's hand and pointing to the boats at the pier.

"You know Carol and I could never have kids. We talked about adopting a few times, but I was so busy with my career I didn't think it would be fair to a child. It wasn't until all this happened that I realize it would have been nice to have a child in our life; especially now."

Here's my chance, Margo thought seeing the sadness move over his face. She cleared her throat trying to find the right words, but there was no right way to deliver this news.

The sun retreated behind a bank of clouds darkening their corner of the room.

"Rick, I need to tell you something." She looked down, twisting her napkin in her lap. "You do have a child. You and I have a child," she blurted out. Lifting her eyes to look at Rick, she suddenly felt like she was going to be sick. She took a big gulp of her iced tea.

"What?" He sat up straight, knocking a knife off the table. The waiter rushed over to pick it up, but Rick waved him away. "What are you talking about?" he asked, his voice rising. Looking around the restaurant, he leaned forward. "What are you saying?"

"After you left for Seattle, I discovered I was pregnant. I was going to tell you. I picked up the phone many times. I didn't know how you'd react," she hurried on before he could speak. "You never made any promises to me about a future or talked about leaving your wife. I didn't want to make you choose me and the baby over your marriage and career." Margo studied his face; it was ashen with the exception of a faint pink blush creeping up his neck. Her throat tightened. She stopped the tears with her napkin. "Honestly, Rick, I didn't want to know if you would choose me."

"Margo, why didn't you tell me?" Rick said through clenched jaw. "We should have made that decision together. I would have taken care of you. You should have given me the chance. How could you think so little of me that you didn't trust me to do right by you?"

"That's just it, Rick. You would have felt you had to do right by me. I wouldn't have known if you did it out of love or duty. Your career would have been ruined. It would have gotten out. People would have talked about me. I was ashamed. I didn't want to be the other woman. I would have lost my job too. And what about what it would have done to Carol? No, I didn't want to be the cause of all that."

"What happened to the baby?" He paused. "You didn't...?"

"No, I would never do that! Why would you even ask that?" She felt the anger rising in her throat. She didn't want to admit to herself that she had considered it for a brief moment. "I took a leave of absence and went to a place in Denver for unwed mothers. After I had the baby, I gave her up for adoption. Rick, you never gave me any indication you would leave your marriage for me. We never even talked about it. Honestly, I don't even know if I wanted you to. I knew how much your career meant to you. I didn't want you to jeopardize it," she said defensively, trying to hold back the tears. "I didn't want to be the one responsible for you losing your wife and career. And, truthfully, I was only twenty-three. I wasn't ready to be a mother. It wasn't an easy decision to make, but I did what I thought was best for me and the baby."

"You said her. It was a girl? Do you know who adopted her? Was it a good family?" His face was tight. The pink on his neck turned darker and crept across his fair cheeks.

"Rick, I've missed her every day. I can't tell you how many times I wanted to call and tell you, but what good would it have done? I'm only telling you right now because she may be in trouble."

"Trouble? What do you mean, trouble? Have you known where she was all this time?" he asked, his voice rising again.

"No, I just started looking for her recently. My nephew, Eric, is a law student. He helped me with the search. Her name is Aimee Gordon. He found out she was adopted by an upper middle-class family in Ventura. Her father is the vice president of a bank and her mother is some kind of socialite." Margo felt the tears welling up, blurring her vision of Rick.

He reached across the table and took her hand. "I didn't mean to upset you. I'm just in shock," his tone softening. "You said she could be in trouble. What kind of trouble?"

"Aimee disappeared from her home a week ago. The only reason I know about it is her parents gave my name to the police thinking she might have contacted me or that I might have something to do with her disappearance. I didn't, of course, but apparently they thought Aimee was trying to find me," Margo rushed on. "At first, the police thought she might have been taken by a human trafficking ring. You know, they look for runaways and make them think they're going to help them. That's still a possibility, but they know now she's in the company of a young man she met on a trip to Thailand with her parents. Apparently, after she returned to the States, they began emailing each other and planned to run away together. Now, he's taken her back to Thailand," Margo stifled sobs in her napkin. "Seems she's in love with him and went willingly."

"Oh my God, I can't believe this. Isn't it considered kidnapping?" Rick said.

"No, she's eighteen. She's beautiful, Rick." Margo reached into her purse and handed him the picture of Aimee that Sam had given her.

"She looks just like you did when we met. Oh, Margo, I wish you hadn't gone through all of this alone. We could have worked something out. You should have trusted me. I did, still do, love you, you know. Wow, I have a daughter!" He said, handing the photo to her and sinking back in his chair. "What can I do to help?"

"Well, Sam says the FBI can't get involved until they have some kind of proof that she didn't go willingly or that she's in some danger," Margo said, trying to ignore what he said about loving her.

"Sam? Who's Sam?"

"He's the police detective who's assigned to the case. He's been very kind and has made it a priority. He's waiting on background information on this young man that she's with. Oh, Rick, it's such a mess. I really thought I was doing the right thing. I wasn't going to tell you today, but then you talked about not having children and, well, I had to tell you."

Suddenly, all the feelings she had buried washed over her. She was glad she told him. A part of her wanted him to share her fear. Yes, it was her choice not to tell him about the pregnancy, but now he knew. It helped that he was beginning to suffer some of the pain of loss she had endured all these years.

"I'm not going back to Seattle tonight," Rick said decisively. "I want to talk to this detective. I have connections in Thailand. There's got to be something I can do."

"Are you sure? This is all you need when you're still grieving the loss of Carol."

"I'm sure. I want to be here for you and our daughter. I need to be able to do something."

"Okay, I'll call him in the morning and see when he can see us," Margo said. Her mind was racing. She needed to talk to Sam before that meeting. They had never talked about why she had given Aimee up or anything about the birth father; now he was going to meet Rick.

"Would you like to go for a drive or something?" Rick asked, waving to the waiter for their bill. "There's much more we need to talk about."

"What? No, I'm sorry, Rick, I can't stay. I have plans. I'll call you in the morning and let you know what time we can go to the police station." She knew he was upset by this news, feeling lonely and still grieving, but she wasn't ready to provide the shoulder he needed right now, and she didn't want his. She felt an odd mix of anger and compassion for him. *How can I be angry with him? He didn't know about the baby.* Now, she wondered what might have happened if she had told him? *Could we have been a family? Maybe Aimee wouldn't have run away. Maybe she wouldn't be in danger now.*

As soon as she returned from the brunch, she pulled out Sam's card and dialed his private number written on the back.

"Sam? It's Margo. I'm sorry to bother you on a Sunday. Can you meet me for a cup of coffee or something? It's important."

"What's wrong? Are you okay?"

"I'm okay. I need to tell you something. It has to do with Aimee."

"I can meet you at Johnnies Coffee Shop on Wilshire in about an hour. Is that okay?"

"Yes, thanks so much."

When Margo walked into the coffee shop, Sam could see the strain on her face. She gave him a small smile.

"Let me get you a latte," he said, waving to the waitress. "What's going on?"

Margo slid into her chair and, this time, she reached over and covered his warm, strong hand with hers. She inhaled deeply and fixed her eyes on his. "I need to tell you why I gave Aimee up for adoption because you are about to meet her birth father."

"What? He's here?" Sam asked, quickly scanning the coffee shop.

"No, no, but he's in town. He wants to talk to you about Aimee's disappearance. Sam, do you remember the friend whose wife died and the memorial I attended?"

"Yes."

"He and I worked together at the airport. I was in my twenties. He was my boss; he was married. We didn't mean for it to happen. We both knew it wasn't right, but we fell in love. I guess that's what everyone in that situation says," she said ruefully.

"And he left you when you got pregnant?" Sam asked, setting his jaw.

"Oh no, it wasn't like that. He didn't know about Aimee. Right after he was promoted and moved to Seattle, I found out I was pregnant. He never led me to believe he would leave his wife. We never even talked about it. He was moving up the ladder in the company. I decided not to tell him. I guess I didn't really want to find out if he would choose me over his marriage and career." Margo continued, "And, honestly, I know it must sound awful, but I wasn't ready to be a mother or lose my job. I stopped answering his calls and took a leave of absence to have the baby. I didn't even tell my family. Believe me, I've questioned that decision every day of my life."

"When did you tell him? What did he say?"

"I told him today at lunch. He's in town for his wife's memorial." She added quickly, "Of course, he was shocked. It's a lot to take in. I felt he needed to know, especially now that Aimee may be in trouble. He asked me to make an appointment with you tomorrow for us to come down to the station and talk about the case. He's now a senior vice president in the company and has lots of contacts in Thailand. He thinks he might be able to help. He needs to be able to help." Margo said studying Sam's face for understanding.

Sam leaned back, releasing his hand from hers and clasping his coffee cup so tightly his knuckles turned white.

"And how do you feel about that? About him being involved?"

"That's really up to you, Sam. Rick and his wife never had any children and now that his wife's gone, I think it will really help him to feel he's doing something for Aimee. I guess I robbed him of that chance when I didn't tell him I was pregnant," Margo said sadly. "But it's your call. I just didn't want you to be blindsided."

"Well, he is her father so it's my responsibility to inform all of Aimee's parents. I can see you both at eleven tomorrow morning. Thank you for giving me a heads-up, Margo," he said coolly, as he stood up. "I'll get the check. See you tomorrow."

She hadn't been sure how Sam would react to all of this. She couldn't blame him if he didn't want to have anything more to do with her outside of the case. Suddenly, Margo felt very alone.

CHAPTER 20

AIMEE

When they boarded the plane, Kris put his hand on the small of Aimee's back and guided her to the second row of first class. For a brief moment, she wondered how he could afford such a luxury. She was, of course, accustomed to flying first class with her parents. After all, her father was a man of means and they were usually travelling on the bank's dime, but in the flurry of settling in and the swift appearance of the flight attendant, she forgot to ask Kris.

"Welcome aboard Mr. Montri, Miss Gordon. What can I get you to drink?"

Aimee glanced at Kris.

"How about some champagne," he responded, "to celebrate our engagement."

"With pleasure and congratulations."

As the plane lifted into the evening dusk, Aimee peered at the glittering lights of Los Angeles. She attributed the pinging of her heart against her chest and the queasy feeling in her stomach to the motion of the plane and Kris's breath on her neck as he leaned over to share the view.

"To us," he said, touching his glass to hers, "and to being together at last."

Aimee glanced down at the cubic zirconia ring he had surprised her with the night before.

"I'll get you a real diamond when we get to Bangkok," he said, when he slipped it on her left hand, "but this will do for now while we're travelling together."

"It's very pretty, but it will be fun to pick out our real rings together," she said, holding up her hand and admiring it. "I love an emerald cut with baguettes on each side and white gold, of course."

"Of course, whatever you want," Kris said.

A couple of hours into the flight, her stomach had not settled down. It didn't help that Kris had slipped on the sleeping mask provided in their first-class kit and was now miles away in la-la land. She really wanted to talk about the wedding and when she could get in touch with her parents to let them know she was okay. *They're probably very worried,* she thought, at least, she hoped so. *Maybe now they'll understand how I felt when they lied to me about who I really am.* It had been two days since she had left her home. Kris cautioned her not to get in touch with them. He said they might try to stop them.

"The police won't get involved because you're eighteen, and by the time they decide to investigate, we'll be in Bangkok and you can email them. I'm going to take good care of you," he assured her.

The memory of that assurance, his leg pressed against hers and his head resting on her shoulder made her push any second thoughts away.

After deplaning, Kris hurried her along towards the line for Immigration.

"Do you have your passport out?"

"Yes, I have it right here."

"When they ask you the purpose of your visit, tell them it's for pleasure and that you're only in the country for two weeks. Don't mention that we're getting married."

"But why?" Aimee asked, furrowing her brow.

"Trust me, they'll ask a lot of questions and it will take forever to get through."

Exiting Immigration, Kris steered her quickly through baggage claim and Customs to the now familiar black town car. This time he climbed into the back seat with her as the driver loaded their luggage into the trunk.

Leaning over, he kissed her on the cheek and extended his hand. "Give me your passport. You won't need it here and I don't want you to lose it."

Aimee fished it out of her purse and handed it to him.

"I'm going to take you to stay with my friend, Pim, until our wedding. You know our customs are very different than in America. It would not be proper for me to take you to my apartment. We must protect your reputation."

"When will I get to see you? Be with you? How long before we can get married?" Aimee asked, feeling anxious again.

"Naturally, I have a lot of arranging to do. Pim will help you with the wedding plans. You can go shopping for your dress and I'll see you every evening. You're going to have a good time with her. She can teach you all you need to know about our customs," Kris said, as he put his arm around her, tipped her chin up and kissed her. "You do know I love you, don't you?"

"Yes, and I love you," she said dreamily resting her head on his shoulder. "I can't wait to be your wife. When can I get in touch with my parents? They must be worried."

"I'll send them an email from the office tomorrow to let them know you're okay, but we won't tell them about the wedding until afterward. They can come see us after we're married."

When Aimee decided to run away with Kris, it had all seemed very romantic. She hadn't thought about her parents not being at her wedding, and her father not giving her away. Or that her friends, especially Debbie, would not be there either. There would be no bridal shower or bachelorette party. And, really, they had almost started the honeymoon. Once again, she pushed the anxious thoughts away. *I really love this beautiful man. I will belong to him. He'll take care of me. This will be a wonderful story to tell our children, much better than the average wedding tale.*

Aimee liked Pim immediately. She was dressed in a green silk kimono when she opened the door. Her ebony hair hung down her back in a loose braid. She had that exotic beauty associated with Thai women.

"Welcome," she said, slightly bowing to Aimee and then Kris.

Her apartment was elegantly furnished with traditional carved teak tables and silk-upholstered chairs. One wall of the apartment was mirrored to reflect the view from the large windows across the room. It was night in Bangkok and the city lights winked at Aimee. She remembered how much she loved this place.

"I'm sure you're tired," Kris said, setting her Louis Vitton bag on the floor. "I'll leave you two to get acquainted and get some sleep. I'll see you tomorrow evening for dinner." He kissed her and was gone.

Aimee started to protest as he closed the door.

"Are you hungry?" Pim asked. "I have some rice and chicken I can heat up."

"Thank you, but I didn't get much sleep on the plane. I hope you don't mind if I just take a shower and go to bed."

"Not at all. I'll show you your room. The guest bathroom is right across the hall. I've laid out some towels for you." Pim picked up Aimee's bag and led her down a hallway to the guest bedroom.

Aimee hadn't realized how tired she was until she showered and put on her nightgown. As she headed across the hall to the bedroom, she heard the phone ring. She stopped and leaned her head toward the living room thinking it might be Kris for her, but Pim was speaking in Thai. The only thing she understood was the name Huron. *Huron is the man I met when I came to Bangkok. The man who made me uncomfortable. The man who didn't bring his wife. How does Pim know him? I'll have to ask her in the morning.*

CHAPTER 21

MARGO

Margo's anxiety was high as she headed to her appointment with Sam and Rick. *I can't believe this is all happening. Rick back in my life, our child in danger, and meeting a man like Sam who makes me feel hopeful and desirable. And now he may not feel that way anymore. How did my life get so complicated?*

She glanced at herself in the mirror on her closet door. Margo, the bag lady, no longer stared back at her. But she wasn't Margurite either. *Who am I really? I'm certainly not the Margo Rick fell in love with. Too many years have gone by for both of us. Am I the Margo Sam kissed?* "Who are you really?" she asked the girl in the mirror.

When Margo entered the precinct waiting room, she could see Rick already seated in Sam's office. Spotting her through the window, Sam rose from his chair and opened his office door to motion her in.

"Thank you for coming, Miss Kitteridge," he said, sounding very formal. "Mr. Cathcart just arrived."

"Please, call me Rick," Rick said, rising from his chair and attempting to give Margo a peck on the cheek.

"Hi, Rick. You got here early," Margo said, turning her head quickly to avoid his kiss. "Detective," she said, extending her hand to Sam, "call me Margo."

She hoped Sam could see the question in her eyes. She wished she could tell if "they" were okay. He wasn't cold, but he wasn't warm either.

"I was just telling Mr. Cathcart, Rick, that Aimee's parents received an email from Aimee telling them that she's safe and with Kris. She said they're in love and plan to marry. They told me they didn't think it sounded like Aimee and it wasn't sent from her email address. Naturally, her parents are upset. They're making arrangements to go to Bangkok to see her and try to talk her out of it."

"So does that mean that she's not involved in any sex trafficking ring and that it's just a case of young love?" Rick asked hopefully.

"I'd like to think that's the case; however, some things don't add up. We've discovered that Kris Montri works for a man named Mano Huron, who is the owner of a large silk-manufacturing company in Bangkok. Further, this Mr. Huron is being investigated for drug trafficking by the Thai authorities, but they don't have enough evidence yet to make an arrest."

"Is the FBI involved in the investigation?" Margo asked. "I know there was some question if they would be called since Aimee is eighteen and it looks like she went willingly."

"Well, they aren't involved in it officially because, as you said, there doesn't seem to be any evidence of kidnapping. However, my friends at the Bureau got the information about the drug investigation from Interpol," Sam said.

"Are you saying there's nothing you can do for Aimee?" Rick asked, his voice rising a little.

"Unfortunately, I have no authority to continue the investigation on the part of the LAPD and it looks like the FBI won't be pursuing it," Sam said, sounding defensive. "Personally, though, I'd like to continue to help. I don't like the fact that the Gordons don't believe the email was from Aimee. Montri's actions fit the profile of a human trafficker. You both probably have heard a little about how pimps work and stories about how they control the girls through fear and intimidation, and yes, abuse." He focused his eyes on

Margo. "What makes it hard for us to help them is the girls think they've found someone who really loves them. They do a good job of isolating the girls from access to family and friends. The people involved in human trafficking are much the same. However, I want you both to understand that it's about economics rather than sex. These people are making big money off of the sex trade and many times, they're working for people in high powered positions like this Mr. Huron," Sam said, and then stopped as he noticed the tears well up in Margo's eyes. "I'm so sorry, Margo," he said softly. "I don't mean to upset you, but you need to know that Aimee could still be in danger."

"I know people in Bangkok, Kitt," Rick said quickly, leaning over and putting his arm around the back of Margo's chair. "I can't just sit by and wonder if she's okay. I'm going over there. Do you want to come with me?"

Before Margo could answer, Sam jumped in. "Who are your contacts? You don't want to mess with these people. You could both get hurt or, worse yet, put Aimee in more danger. Look, I can't do anything officially, but if you intend to go there, I can put you in touch with an old friend of mine over there who might be able to help you. His name is Joe McCallister. He retired from the Drug Enforcement Administration and is now a private investigator in Bangkok. I already have a call in to him to see if he can do some digging."

"Yes, Rick, I want to go. I can't sit over here wondering what's happening. I didn't do right by Aimee before; I'm not going to let her down again. We can get in touch with Sam's friend and see how we can help. Let me put in for time off. I can probably leave the day after tomorrow, but you should go ahead. Besides, I don't want any rumors to start if we're seen travelling together," Margo said, quickly glancing at Sam.

"Detective, do you know what the Gordons' plans are? Maybe we should try to work together on this," Rick said.

"That's probably a good idea. If Montri is involved in human trafficking and has targeted Aimee, we don't want him to know we're onto him or it will be difficult to find her. Right now, he probably thinks her parents are his only problem. Shall I call them and set up a meeting?" Sam looked at Margo. "Is that okay with you, Margo? I know it might be tough for you."

He really does still care, Margo thought. "Yes, it's what we need to do. Anything for Aimee."

Margo turned to Rick. "Let's not tell them you're Aimee's father. They might make an unfair judgment about you, us, and not want our help."

"That's probably a good idea," Sam quickly agreed. "Just tell them he's your friend."

Margo turned toward Sam and silently mouthed, "Thank you."

"If you think that's best. I can be back here this afternoon after I make my arrangements. I'll leave on the red-eye tonight for Bangkok," Rick said, establishing control.

As Sam dialed the Gordons' number, Margo sucked in her breath. *What are they like? What will they think of me? I need to tell them how grateful I am that they've given Aimee a good life. At least I hope it's been a good life. But she did run away. What's that all about?* She was surprised that she was suddenly glad Rick would be by her side.

CHAPTER 22

The meeting with the Gordons was set for four o'clock that same after-noon in Sam's office. When they arrived, Rick and Margo were already there. Margo was surprised that they looked older than her, probably in their mid-fifties. Then she reminded herself the adoption agency said the couple wanted to adopt because they had been unsuccessful in getting pregnant.

Martin Gordon was distinguished looking with silver hair and a mus-tache. He was a little shorter than Rick's 5'11" and the epitome of a banker in his finely tailored, pinstriped suit. Helen Gordon was slender and stately looking in a purple, long-sleeved sheath dress and pearls. Her silver hair was cut in a layered bob. She seemed to glide into the room. Margo was imme-diately intimidated by her. She tugged on the bottom of her bomber jacket in an attempt to cover the top of her jeans. *I should have let Margurite decide what I would wear.*

"It's good to meet you, Miss Kitteridge," Helen said, extending her hand. "I'm sorry it's under these circumstances. I can see your face in Aimee's."

"I'm sorry, too. Please call me Margo. This is my friend, Rick Cathcart."

As everyone shook hands all around, Margo tried to cover her nerves with a firm handshake. Thankfully, Sam got right down to business.

"Thank you for coming, Mr. and Mrs. Gordon. Please sit down. I told Margo and Rick about the email you received and your concern that it wasn't really from Aimee."

The Gordons sat down in the two chairs next to Margo.

"Yes, it didn't sound at all like her," Helen responded. "For one thing, she made no attempt to explain why she left the way she did. As I told you

Detective, Aimee has been very upset with us because of the way she found out she was adopted." She turned toward Margo. "We made the mistake of not telling Aimee when she was old enough to understand. There just never seemed to be the right moment, and frankly, we didn't want her to stop thinking of us as her parents."

"So all this time Aimee knew nothing about my existence or the reason I gave her up? How did she find out?" Margo felt the heat rising on her neck.

Martin reached over and placed his hand on Helen's arm. "Her mother took her to the doctor for some tests because she was having digestive issues. When the doctor asked for family history, Aimee apparently overheard Helen tell the doctor she couldn't provide much since she was adopted. It was unfortunate. Since then, she's closed down to us. That was one of the reasons we took her with us to Bangkok." He dropped his head down. "We never dreamed she would decide to take off with this young man."

"Actually, she seemed to be much better in Thailand," Helen interjected. "In fact, Martin and I had discussed getting her into counseling when we got home, but she was behaving more and more like herself. We thought she was adjusting." Helen retrieved a handkerchief from her purse and blotted under her eyes being careful not to smudge her makeup.

"Do you still think Aimee is in some kind of danger?" Martin asked, his brow furrowing. "It's not just a case of her being love struck?"

"I certainly hope so, but it concerns me that we now know that this Kris Montri works for a man named Huron, who owns a silk factory there and has some suspicious business connections."

"We met Mr. Huron at Mr. Anon's home! He's on the board of the bank," Martin exclaimed. "You don't think he has anything to do with Aimee's disappearance, do you?"

"That's what we need to find out. Since the LAPD isn't prepared to take the case any further, I can't officially do anything more. However, I do want to continue to help in an unofficial role."

"We just need to get over there and talk some sense into her," Helen stated. "We spent a lot of time with Kris; he seemed like such a nice young man. I can't believe he could be involved in anything as horrific as human trafficking. I feel it's just a case of romantic infatuation on Aimee's part. That's why Martin and I are planning to leave for Bangkok tomorrow."

"My concern, Mrs. Gordon, is that if Mr. Montri's intentions are not on the up and up, and if he thinks you're going to mess up his plans, you may not be able to find him or Aimee," Sam hesitated. "He'll go underground, as we say."

For a moment, Helen seemed to lose her cool composure. She reached for Martin's hand. "But we can't just sit here and do nothing!"

"We feel the same way," Margo said. "That's why Rick and I want to help."

"Yes, we both work for an airline and I have connections in Bangkok who might be able to help," Rick said. "Mr. and Mrs. Gordon, I understand your concern and need to take action," he said in his most persuasive voice, "but let us have a day to see what we can find out. This Montri guy doesn't know us and won't even know we're connected to Aimee. We'll keep you informed through Detective Carpenter and you can come over in a couple of days."

Sam leaned forward, propped his elbows on his desk, and clasped his hands. "I'm proposing that you delay your trip for a few days until Rick and Margo can do some digging in Bangkok. I have a friend who is a private investigator there who will help them."

"That makes sense; we sure don't want him to suspect anything and take off with Aimee, or worse yet, harm her," Martin said, looking to Helen for agreement.

"All right but we do need to answer the email or he'll be suspicious. What do you suggest we say, Detective?"

"Tell Aimee you miss her, and you're concerned about her. Ask her to put the wedding off until you can arrange to come over there. Tell her you want to be part of the wedding planning, and her father wants to be there to give her away. Tell her you'll be there by the weekend. That will give Rick and Margo time, with the help of my friend, to locate her. Who knows, maybe he really does love her and will be willing to have you be part of their plans," Sam said encouragingly.

"I want to thank you both for loving Aimee and giving her such a good life," Margo said, struggling to hold back her tears. "I did what I thought was best for her. I've thought of her every day since she was born. I want you to know I never would have tried to talk to her or see her without you knowing it."

"I appreciate that, Miss Kitteridge. She's been a real gift to us," Helen said, rising and clasping Margo's hand in both of hers. "Please be careful. I hope we can get her back with us as soon as possible. And, that our biggest problem will be to talk her out of marrying right now."

"Thank you for your help, Mr. Cathcart," Martin said, shaking Rick's hand. "I hope our fears are unfounded."

"So do I," Rick replied, studying the man who had been a father to his child. "We'll stay in touch through Detective Carpenter. We'll see you in Bangkok in a few days, hopefully with Aimee."

CHAPTER 23

AIMEE

When Aimee awoke the next morning, she was confused for a moment. Looking around the room, memories of the flight to Bangkok and Kris leaving her with Pim flooded back. A blue silk kimono lay at the bottom of the bed. Wrapping it around her, she stuffed her feet into her sandals and made her way down the hall.

"You're up. How did you sleep?" Pim greeted Aimee when she entered the small kitchen. "I wasn't sure what you like for breakfast. I have some fruit and pastries. Would you like some coffee?"

"That's fine, thanks," Aimee answered, suppressing a yawn. "I slept well. What time is it?"

"It's almost noon. I'm glad you were able to sleep. It will help with the jet lag if you can get on our time. You can just relax today. Kris won't be here until around seven tonight."

Aimee slid onto a high, wicker stool at the bar. Pim leaned across the counter and placed a plate of mango and papaya cut in half, along with what looked to be orange slices. When Aimee placed a slice in her mouth, she was surprised to find it tasted like grapefruit.

"What's this?"

"That's pomelo. Do you like it?" Pim responded, slicing open a strange red fruit with spikes on it. "I'm fixing you some dragon fruit as well. It comes from a cactus plant."

"It looks like kiwi. I like kiwi, except for the seeds."

Aimee recognized the bowl of sticky rice Pim offered her. She had enjoyed it on her previous trip to Bangkok. It reminded her of the dinner with Kris at Mr. Anon's house. "So, how do you know Kris?" she asked, blowing on the steaming mug of coffee.

Pim slid onto the seat beside Aimee. "Kris and I work for Mr. Huron. I believe you met him when you were here with your parents. I am the marketing manager for his silk factory."

"I thought Kris worked for the bank. He was our tour guide on our trip."

"Since Mr. Huron is on the board, Kris sometimes does guide work for the bank. He tells me you two are going to be married. That's very exciting," Pim said, changing the subject. "I'll be happy to teach you about our wedding customs. We can go shopping for a dress for you. It'll be fun. Now eat your breakfast." Stepping down from the bar stool, she pointed toward the living room. "There are some books on the coffee table you might want to look through. You can take your shower after me."

CHAPTER 24

MAC

Joe McCallister, or Mac as his friends called him, sat outside the posh high-rise apartment building in Bangkok waiting for Kris Montri to come out. He had watched Kris arrive home an hour earlier, around three o'clock. Mac was of average height and weight except for a slight paunch that had come with retirement. His thick head of silver hair, easy smile, and blue eyes projected a kind, fatherly appearance. He didn't fit one's image of a DEA agent, let alone a private investigator. It was only when you looked directly into those eyes that you saw the strength and resolve that had struck fear in many a felon. When his old friend, Sam, called to ask for help in finding a missing girl, he let Mac know he had more than a professional interest in the case. Mac's research found that, while Montri was employed by Huron Textiles, he was trying to become an actor and had even done some modeling, but he certainly wasn't making enough money to afford this high-priced address.

Sam told him about the investigation into Huron's business dealings, but Mac learned early on he couldn't trust anyone in Bangkok law enforcement. So, he gathered what information he could from his buddies at the Drug Enforcement Administration housed in the American Embassy. They suspected Huron of being involved in drug trafficking into the U.S. and sex trafficking that catered to some very powerful figures in Bangkok society. Although they couldn't officially get involved in Aimee's case, they agreed to help Mac with any information they came upon that might shed some light on Huron's involvement.

Mac straightened up in the seat when he saw Montri exit his building and get into a waiting black town car. He slowly pulled away from the curb, following at a safe distance. They made a stop at a flower stall and then at another high-rise apartment building. Mac slid into a parking space behind the town car. When the town car pulled away, he lifted his binoculars and watched Kris push the call button on the bottom right side of the brass panel at the entrance. He pushed the heavy glass door and entered the building. Mac slid out of his car, and taking a quick look around, approached the entrance. The name by the call button read 'Pim Sakda'. He jotted it down in his notepad, and returned to his car.

CHAPTER 25

AIMEE

When she heard the doorbell ring, Aimee rushed to open it. Kris was carrying a large box. Balanced on top of the box was a bouquet of small white flowers with deep yellow centers. He leaned in and kissed Aimee lightly. "For you," he said, motioning for her to take the flowers.

"They smell wonderful," Aimee said, breathing in the sweet scent. "What are they? They're familiar."

"In Thai, we call them *'leelawadee'*. You may know them as plumeria," Pim offered. "They're very popular for weddings. Give them to me and I'll put them in water."

"I'm glad you like them and I hope you will like this," Kris said, handing her the box.

Putting the box on the sofa, she pulled the top off and squealed. She lifted up the red Thai silk sheath embroidered with tiny flowers resembling the plumeria. It had cap sleeves, a mandarin collar, and a slit up one side. It reminded her of the one she had seen in the open market. "Oh, Kris, it's beautiful. Isn't it beautiful, Pim?"

"Go put it on, we're going to a party," Kris laughed.

She nearly dropped the box as she stopped to hug Kris and raced to her bedroom.

"She's a lovely girl. Mr. Huron will be pleased," Pim whispered. "How are you handling the parents?"

"I got an email from them after I sent one as Aimee. They're coming over this weekend to be here for the wedding, but I know they intend to talk her into going back home so I have to move her more quickly than anticipated. I need your help. You must come with us tonight to Huron's party. I need to leave her there, and she'll be more comfortable staying if you're with her. Mano will arrange for you both to fly to his place in Phuket tomorrow with the other girls. I'll tell her I'll join you in a day."

"Won't her parents get the authorities to come after you?" Pim asked.

"I don't think so. They believe that Aimee is in love with me and wants to marry me. I'm sure they think they can talk her out of it. By the time they discover they can't find Aimee and they notify the police, I'll be in Singapore on business and Mano will have delivered her to his client. There'll be no trace of an American girl named Aimee Gordon, and I will have completed my assignment."

"Ah, you look lovely, my darling. Just like a real Thai woman," Kris said, his voice rising when Aimee appeared.

"I love it, Kris. You even brought me shoes," Aimee beamed as her leg peeked through the slit in the dress to reveal gold, strapped high heels. "I love it all," she gushed, flinging her arms around Kris's neck.

"I've convinced Pim to come with us," Kris said. "We're going to a real Thai party."

"I'll be right with you," Pim said, heading down the hallway to her bedroom.

In her room, Pim changed into a peacock blue sheath. Going to a jewelry box on her dresser, she lifted the false bottom and selected a long gold chain with an opal pendant. Putting the necklace over her head, she held the pendant close to her lips and whispered, "Can you hear me?"

"You're good to go," a man's voice answered in Thai.

CHAPTER 26

MAC

Not long after Montri entered the building, another black town car arrived. Mac watched as Montri escorted two women dressed in traditional Thai clothing out to the waiting car. Glancing at the picture of Aimee that Sam had faxed him, he recognized her as the girl in red.

Mac pulled away from the curb and followed the town car to the outskirts of Bangkok to a stately house surrounded by a high iron fence. Guards stood at the gate, peered into the town car, and waved it through. Driving slowly past the gate, Mac peered through his passenger window. He could make out several cars parked along the circular driveway. The first floor was brightly lit and finely dressed people could be seen moving through the entry flanked by white-garbed butlers. Music blended with an array of voices and laughter. Mac continued to the end of the estate grounds, stopped and quickly compared the address to his research notes to verify it was the home of Mano Huron. Knowing what he did about lavish Thai parties, Montri and Aimee weren't going anywhere any time soon. Mac called his partner to meet him at the Huron estate to continue the surveillance. He would come back in a couple of hours, but right now, he needed to get to the Shangri La Hotel to meet up with Rick Cathcart.

CHAPTER 27

RICK

Rick pressed the elevator button for the lobby. He was tired from the flight but the idea that he was on a mission to save his child energized him. He still couldn't comprehend it all. *I have a child. A daughter. And now she might be in trouble.* His feelings for Margo were mixed. She had robbed him of the chance to step up and be a father. He also knew he had been so driven in his career that he probably would have resented having to make such a choice. And it may have even ended his marriage. He couldn't have done that to Carol. *Now, I have the opportunity to do something for Aimee. Maybe even be able to be a father for her.* For the first time in a long time, he felt alive.

"Mr. McCallister, Rick Cathcart," Rick said approaching Mac in the lobby. "Thanks so much for helping us."

"Let's go into the bar, and please, call me Mac."

"I just came from staking out the Huron estate where Miss Gordon is attending a party with Montri," Mac said, sliding into the booth. He waved to the waitress. "I'll have a diet cola. Mr. Cathcart, what will you have?"

"A beer, please, and call me Rick. I really appreciate you helping us. Detective Carpenter spoke very highly of you. My friend Margo will be arriving tomorrow morning. I suppose Sam told you that Margo is Aimee's biological mother. She gave her up for adoption and until recently, she didn't even know where Aimee was until Detective Carpenter called to tell her Aimee was missing," Rick said.

"I found out that this Kris Montri fellow works for Huron's company. As far as I can tell, his job has nothing to do with the textile business," Mac said, leaning forward. "He appears to be some kind of errand boy for Huron. That is, when he's not modeling men's clothing in magazines. I don't know how much he's involved in the shady side of Huron's business dealings, but my gut tells me Aimee was an assignment for Montri."

"What kind of assignment?" Rick asked, suddenly feeling a wave of nausea.

"I don't know, but at the moment, he has her staying in a posh apartment with a woman named Pim Sakda. In the morning, I'll find out who she is and how she fits in. Montri picked them both up and took them to a party at Huron's estate about an hour ago. Thai parties tend to last well into the night, so I'll be back on surveillance before they return to Miss Sakda's apartment. In the meantime, my partner is watching the house."

"I know you're probably wondering what Margo and I can do to help, and frankly, I don't know myself," Rick said. "When I heard that Mano Huron of Huron Textiles might be involved somehow in Aimee's disappearance, I checked and found that they're a big customer of my airline, both in passenger and cargo business. In my position as senior vice president, I may be able to get information on his travel and shipment history or something."

"What time does Miss Kitteridge get in?" Mac asked.

"She'll be in around 8:00 a.m."

"Let's meet here at ten o'clock. By then, I'll have information on Miss Sakda and anything that happens tonight at the party." Mac slid out of the booth and shook Rick's hand. "You get some rest. I'll see you in the dining room in the morning and we'll make a plan."

"Thank you again, Mac. We're really grateful for your help, and of course, I'll be paying you for your services. We have to get Aimee back as soon as we can before anything bad happens to her."

CHAPTER 28

AIMEE

Aimee's eyes widened as they entered the foyer of Huron's estate. The floors were honey-colored marble. A large crystal chandelier hung from a twenty-foot ceiling, casting diamond shapes across the entry. On her left, white marble pillars flanked a sweeping marble staircase with ornate, black wrought iron balusters depicting tropical flowers. It reminded her of a room from *Dynasty,* her favorite TV show.

"Oh, it's so beautiful," Aimee exclaimed as Kris escorted her and Pim through the entrance. "Everyone looks so elegant. Whose house is this?"

"This is the home of Mr. Huron. He is the owner of a large silk factory in Bangkok. His father came to Thailand from France and married his mother who is Thai. He started a silk factory, and Huron inherited the family business. In fact, your dress is made of silk from his factory," Kris said. "Remember, you met him at Mr. Anon's house when you were here with your parents? Most of these people are his business associates."

Yes, I remember the man who kept staring at me across the table that night.

Kris guided them through an archway supported on each side by two more marble pillars into the sea of elegantly dressed guests. Waiters moved through the room carrying trays of champagne and colorful Mai Tais. Oriental rugs delineated seating areas with sofas and high-backed easy chairs upholstered in rich silk patterns featuring the popular colors of creams, golds and reds. A focal point of the room was a black marble fireplace trimmed in a gold-leaf floral pattern. A large mirror over the fireplace reflected the arched windows across the room framed by heavy, gold-striped drapes.

Aimee looked around. There seemed to be far more women than men. While the men appeared to be close to her father's age, the women looked much younger. Pim left them to greet two of the women.

"Come, let's say hello to our host," Kris said, steering her toward Mano Huron standing in a circle of men. Kris extended his hand, "Mr. Huron, please allow me to present Miss Aimee Gordon whom you met when she was here with her parents a couple of months ago."

Aimee remembered thinking the first time she saw him at the Anons' residence that although Mr. Huron was probably in his sixties, he was attractive in a distinguished way. He was taller than most of the men in the room—as tall as Kris. The deep mahogany color of his skin was the perfect canvas for his piercing, dark eyes, his salt and pepper hair, and neatly trimmed, dark beard and mustache. He wore a long-sleeved silk shirt of deep teal, and black linen slacks.

"Of course, welcome to Bangkok and to my home, Miss Gordon," Mr. Huron said, smiling and slightly bowing his head.

"Thank you for inviting me," Aimee said. *Was it her imagination or did his eyes travel quickly over her breasts and hips?* Suddenly, her neck was warm and she felt the same discomfort as she had in the Anons' garden.

"Please enjoy some of our best traditional food and drink," he said, gesturing toward another archway. A rectangular teak table was laden with several white porcelain plates. Some were decorated with radish rosettes and leafy ferns carved from carrots. Others bore skewered chicken satay, green papaya salad, chicken salad wonton cups, shrimp lettuce wraps, classic tiny fish cakes and spring rolls with all manner of sauces for dipping.

Aimee stood with a plate in her hand. The options were overwhelming. She was grateful when Pim joined her and began explaining the various dishes and showing her how they were to be eaten.

"These are some of the dishes that will be served at your wedding reception," she said brightly. "See which ones you prefer."

Hearing the words "wedding reception" eased Aimee's discomfort and reminded her of why she had come to Bangkok with Kris. *He's so handsome and sexy,* she thought as Kris came toward them carrying cocktails, *and he loves me. The girls back home will be so jealous.* She could feel her face flush as he handed her a drink.

"To us, my darling," he said tapping her glass with his.

As the evening went on, the music, the elegant surroundings, the blend of voices speaking in strange languages, the laughter and the delicious cocktails Kris kept bringing her dispelled Aimee's concerns about Mr. Huron, and aside from feeling drowsy, she began to enjoy her first Thai party.

Yawning, Aimee asked Kris, "Should we be leaving? A lot of people are leaving."

"I have a surprise for you. It happens that Mr. Huron has been kind enough to invite us to his home on the island of Phuket so that you can enjoy the beautiful beaches and nightlife. You'll love it," Kris said. "You and Pim will stay here tonight and go on his plane in the morning. I have to get some work done in Bangkok. I'll join you there tomorrow evening."

Aimee suddenly felt anxious again. "What about my clothes? Won't I need a bathing suit? I don't have my makeup. Can't we go back to the apartment and come back tomorrow morning?"

"Mr. Huron will provide us with everything we need," Pim assured her. "You can borrow some of my things until Kris brings yours. I've made this trip before and you'll love it. It's such a beautiful island. We might even find a place for you and Kris to be married over there. What do you think, Kris?"

"That's a great idea. Don't worry, dear, I'll join you tomorrow. In the meantime, you and Pim enjoy the trip," Kris said, smiling at Pim. "Thanks for taking care of my girl."

Kris walked to the door with Aimee, kissed her cheek, and whispered in her ear, "Have a good time. I'll be with you again soon."

"Come," Pim said, "I'll show you your room. And, don't worry, my room is just next door to yours."

CHAPTER 29

PIM

As soon as she settled Aimee into her room and brought her pajamas and a change of clothes for the morning trip, Pim went to her room. She hated lying to Aimee, but one thing was for sure, she wasn't going to let Mano Huron's plans for her come to pass. Pim thought about her little cousin, Sunisa, and why she was here.

A year ago, while Pim was working as a buyer for a large department store in Singapore, she got the call from her uncle. He told her the police found the body of his fifteen-year-old daughter, Sunisa, washed up on a beach in Phuket dead of an apparent overdose. She had disappeared a couple of weeks earlier. Pim was devastated, as was the rest of the family. Especially when her uncle told her that police reported Sunisa had been caught up in a sex trafficking ring through the boy she had been dating.

Pim was incensed by the lack of caring on the part of the police. Although they had known of the boy's dealings in the drug and sex trade, they had neglected to intervene in order to investigate the "bigger fish". She was also aware of long-held rumors of police corruption. She had a child-hood friend, Sud, in the department whom she knew she could trust. When she told him about Sunisa, he shared that he was heading up an undercover unit investigating the involvement of Mano Huron in drug trafficking and human trafficking. When he confirmed that Huron's people had probably been responsible for Sunisa's death, Pim was livid. At first, Sud rejected Pim's desire to help due to concern for her safety, but in the end, she convinced him she could really be useful by going undercover in Huron's company.

After Sunisa's funeral, Pim returned to Singapore, quit her job, and moved back to Bangkok. Because of her qualifications, she had no trouble getting a position at Huron's company. It wasn't long before she became a valued employee and was invited to her first party at Huron's estate. It was when he invited her to a business meeting in Phuket that she knew he trusted her.

While visiting Huron's villa in Phuket, she discovered a wing of the house off the main living room that consisted of a long corridor flanked by six rooms on each side. Sud warned her to be aware of hidden cameras so when she saw the small flashing red light at the far end of the corridor, she turned and strolled to the other side of the house where she was staying. That was when Sud gave her the device hidden in the locket.

There were always young girls at the house in Phuket and many of Huron's business associates came and went daily. In the evening, there would be lavish parties and one by one, the girls would disappear down the corridor with a male guest. It made Pim sick to think about her cousin being in this house and what these men must have done to her. What they were doing to these young girls. Huron's arrest couldn't come soon enough.

Now, as Pim sat on the bed surrounded by the extravagance of Mano Huron's estate, she began to weep again as she thought of Sunisa. She looked at the tiny flashing red light of the camera near the ceiling and turning away from it, quickly wiped her tears. She mustn't fall apart now or attract suspicion. She was so close.

She rose from the bed and went into the marble-clad bathroom and turned on the shower. Turning her back, she pressed the pendant to her mouth and whispered in Thai. "We're headed for Phuket on Huron's plane tomorrow morning. Aimee's with us. Kris won't be there. He said his job is done and he's headed to Singapore."

"Got it," the man replied in Thai.

CHAPTER 30

MARGO

Margo settled into the first class seat. *How did all of this happen? I'm on my way to Bangkok to meet my ex-lover and save our child. Then there's Sam. When I'm with him, I feel more like Margo than I have since before Aimee.* She reclined her seat and closed her eyes. *Right now, I need to concentrate on getting Aimee back safe and sound.*

When she arrived at the hotel, Rick met her in the lobby. He gave her a brief hug. After instructing the bellman to take her bag up to her room, he linked her arm through his in the old, familiar way and steered her toward the restaurant.

"Mac, the detective, is meeting us here in a few minutes to fill us in on what he's found out about Aimee. Are you hungry? Were you able to rest on the flight?"

"I got some rest. I just need some coffee and a coconut bun and I'll be fine."

Margo had just taken a bite out of her bun when Rick rose slightly and waved to a tan, casually dressed man with silver hair.

"Margo, this is Joe McCallister."

"Call me Mac. Good to meet you although I'm sorry for the circumstances," Mac said, offering his hand across the table and quickly sliding into the seat across from Margo.

Mac filled Margo in on what he knew about Kris Montri and his relationship with Mano Huron. He told her about seeing him bring Aimee to Pim Sakda's apartment and about their trip to the party at Huron's estate.

"My partner and I staked out the place all night. After the party broke up, Montri left and Aimee and the Sakda woman stayed. This morning, they left with some other women in Huron's private plane headed for Phuket," Mac said. "My partner has gone over to set up a stake out on Huron's villa."

"Do we know if Aimee is okay? You know, has she been hurt in any way?" Margo asked, trying to control the fear in her voice.

"She didn't appear to be doing anything against her will," Mac said. "When they left for the party, both women were dressed to the nines and laughing."

"Who is this woman she's staying with?" Rick asked.

"From what I can find out, she was a highly successful businesswoman in Singapore before she returned to Bangkok and went to work for Huron. She has family here," Mac said. "My friends at the DEA only know about the investigation into Huron's business dealings, but they hadn't heard her name associated with it."

"What's the plan?" Margo asked.

"We need to get someone we can trust into his house in Phuket and make contact with Aimee," Mac said.

"I think I might have an idea," Rick said. "What if I get our local cargo manager to set up a friendly visit for me to thank Huron for his business? I could bring Margo along as my associate."

"That might work," Mac said, "but we'll need to figure out how you can get Aimee out of there without arousing suspicion. It would really be best if you could get invited to a party rather than just a one-on-one meeting so you could mingle and look around."

"I'll talk to our cargo manager and see if he can get me an invite on the pretext of wanting to enjoy a real Thai party while I'm here. After all, I am his senior vice president, he'll probably do anything to impress me," Rick said self- assuredly.

"Okay, but how are we going to get Aimee out of there?" Margo asked.

"Rick tells me you're Aimee's birth mother. Does she know you?" Mac asked.

"No, I gave Aimee up for adoption when she was born. Rick and I are her biological parents, but Rick didn't even know he had a child until I told him a few days ago." Mac shot a look at Rick.

Margo rushed on. "Sam, Detective Carpenter, phoned me when she went missing. She doesn't know anything about me. Apparently her adoptive parents thought she might have found me and ran away to be with me"

"Do you think you're too close to all of this to be able to get her out without anyone being hurt?"

"We'll be very careful and follow any advice you have for us, but we must be able to help her," Rick said reaching over and covering Margo's hand with his. "This is our chance to be there for her."

Margo gave Rick a look of gratitude as she felt shame and affection warm her neck.

"Since she doesn't know us, maybe we can get her to tell us what she thinks is going on. You know, as one American to another," Margo suggested. "If she's frightened, maybe she'll confide in me."

"Well, I'm not crazy about it, but it's the best plan we have under the circumstances. I'll let Sam know what's going on and see if he has any more information for us. Rick, let me know as soon as you get the invitation. In the meantime, my partner and I will keep an eye on everything, but you need to make it happen soon. Who knows what they have planned!"

Mac rose and shook hands with Rick and Margo.

"Thank you so much for all your help, Mac," Margo said, her brown eyes slightly misty as she squeezed his hand.

CHAPTER 31

AIMEE

Aimee was nervous but excited when they boarded Mano Huron's private plane. She felt like one of the celebrities in her magazines when the uniformed flight attendant settled them into the plush leather seats and offered them champagne and a plate of fruit and cheese. Besides Aimee and Pim, there were three other girls on the flight. One seemed to be around Aimee's age. The other two looked to be much younger in spite of their heavy makeup, tight tops barely containing their breasts, and short skirts. As she watched them chatter in a language she didn't understand, Aimee thought one of them seemed familiar. *She's the girl who approached Kris when Mother and I were at the temple. That's strange. Kris said the girl was just a beggar.*

"Who are these girls?" Aimee whispered to Pim.

"Oh, they're friends of Mr. Huron's clients. He often invites them to come to Phuket for some sun and fun."

"I can't wait to see Kris. I miss him so much."

"He should be here tonight," Pim assured her. "In the meantime, enjoy this adventure. Look at that beautiful view."

When they stepped off the plane in Phuket, there were two limousines waiting on the tarmac. Pim led Aimee toward the first one. Two large men who had been on the plane with them steered the other girls into the second one.

As the limousines climbed a narrow road through lush tropical foliage, Aimee glimpsed the gleaming sapphire Andaman Sea below and to her left. Rounding a curve, she caught sight of the villa. It consisted of three levels capped by blue-tiled pagoda roofs marching down a secluded hillside to a sandy beach. The limousines pulled up to the second level. They all climbed out and stepping onto the covered porch, removed their shoes, and placed them on woven bamboo mats. Entering the living room, Aimee could see floor-to-ceiling sliding-glass doors on the other side that opened onto a terrace. In stark contrast to the estate in Bangkok, the interior furnishings were casual and inviting. Rattan sided, upholstered sectional sofas in cream and taupe languished about on the teak floors. Teak deck chairs with blue, taupe, and white-striped cushions sat on the terrace. Once again, Aimee had the feeling she had just stepped into a movie set.

A butler greeted the women. "Mr. Huron bids you welcome. He will be arriving tomorrow morning to prepare for the party. We will show you to your rooms where you can change. There you will find bathing suits, beachwear, and loungewear. Please make yourselves comfortable. We will be serving lunch in an hour." He raised his hand and two young men came quickly to pick up their luggage. He directed Aimee and Pim to follow him down a hall on their left. The two big men pushed the three girls to the right through an open door leading to a long corridor.

"If you like, we can change into our swimwear and I'll show you the beach before lunch," Pim said.

"That will be great. This place is so beautiful. You were right, I'm glad I got to come."

After they explored the grounds and the beach, one of the servants descended the stairs to the pool to tell them lunch was served. Pim led Aimee to the terrace where a small table for two was set with blue-rimmed white plates filled with shrimp-topped Thai noodles. Blue bowls held fried rice with pork and vegetables, green papaya salad and Thai fruits. A knife and spoon as well as chopsticks lay beside the dishes. Pim picked up the chopsticks and expertly lifted a shrimp to her mouth.

"I'm not very good at chopsticks," Aimee said.

"That's okay. You can use the silverware, or if you like, I can teach you how to use the chopsticks. Depends on how hungry you are," laughed Pim.

"I think the sea air has made me too hungry to handle a lesson right now. Why aren't we eating with the other girls?"

"They don't speak English and I'm too hungry to translate for you right now. After lunch, we can relax on the beach if you'd like. It's a beautiful day for a dip in the ocean or the pool."

That evening, a light dinner of Thai chicken, green curry soup, and spring rolls was again set on the terrace table.

"Looks like we might have a monsoon coming," remarked Pim. "See how the waves are becoming rough? Do you know about monsoons?"

"We don't have them where I live in California, but I've seen them on our trip to Arizona. I don't like them. They can be very scary. The winds get fierce and kick up dust that gives the sky a strange orange glow and then the rains come in torrents. Are they like that here?"

"The rains are heavy and the sea is angry with dangerous rip currents so you don't want to be swimming then. It can be bad on the other side of the island." Pim reached over, patted Aimee's arm. "Don't worry, I'll protect you."

Just then, the sky darkened and the wind whipped rain onto the terrace. They squealed, jumped up and scurried into the living room laughing. Aimee could see the girls seated at a table in the kitchen. They had been joined by two other girls. The girl from the temple looked straight at Aimee and then turned her head toward the butler.

That night, unable to sleep, Aimee pulled on her robe and padded bare-foot down the hall from her room into the living room and through the open terrace doors. The terrace overlooked a gleaming, tiled pool surrounded by tented cabanas whose canvas drapes could be closed for privacy. The earlier monsoonal weather had passed them by. Below the pool area, the pristine sand beach stretched toward white-capped waves gently moving in and out. The scent of the sea and the warm breeze made her homesick.

Muffled voices emanated from the corridor on the other side of the room. Curious, Aimee tiptoed across the room. The door to the corridor was slightly ajar. She quietly pushed it open. A soft red glow peeked under closed doors. She thought she heard whimpering and smelled something sweet that was vaguely familiar. She was startled by a large figure approaching her from the other end of the corridor. Instinctively, she began backing out. The beam of a flashlight struck her face and she was momentarily blinded. A huge man dressed in black came into focus. He towered over her.

"What you doing here? Go to your room," he menaced in broken English.

Behind him, a door opened slightly, bathing the end of the corridor in red.

Turning his head, he growled, "Get back inside and shut the door."

Frightened, Aimee turned and quickly crossed to her side of the house. Climbing into bed, she pulled the covers up to her chin. She was shaking. That sweet smell lingered in her nose and transported her to the time one of the boys at school brought her to a party at a beach house. Everyone was drinking heavily; smoke filled the room. Aimee had been offered marijuana once, but she didn't like the smell and didn't like the way people who smoked it acted afterward. When she saw couples disappearing up the stairs and down the halls, she asked the boy to take her home. Although he protested, the offer of a make-out session in the car persuaded him to leave.

Turning on her side in a fetal position and clutching her pillow, Aimee began to cry. For a moment, she forgot she was angry with her mother and wished she could hug her. *It'll be okay as soon as Kris gets here.*

The small red light flashed near the ceiling.

CHAPTER 32

SAM

"There's a Mac McAllister on the phone for you, Detective," the clerk said, leaning into the half-open door at the precinct.

"Mac, good to hear from you. What've you found out? Did Margo get there all right? Have you located Aimee?" the questions poured out of Sam.

"Hang on, brother," Mac said, "take a breath."

"Sorry, Mac, it's just that I'd rather be over there working this case with you."

"I understand. Well, I met with Rick and Margo this morning. Last night, I followed Kris Montri, Aimee, and a woman named Pim Sakda out to Huron's estate. The two women stayed there last night and left on Huron's plane this morning for his villa in Phuket. Aimee seemed to go of her own free will."

"Who is this Pim Sakda?"

"Well, it's odd, Sam. She's a successful business woman who returned to Bangkok from Singapore a year ago and went to work for Huron. DEA has nothing on her as it relates to the investigation. I have a call in to a friend of mine in the Royal Thai Police. I trust him and am hoping he can tell me who she is and how she's involved in any of this."

"How is Margo taking all of this? Do you really think they'll be able to help?"

"Well, Cathcart is trying to get an invitation for them to attend a party at the villa. Apparently, Huron's company is a big client of his airline. He's going on the pretext of thanking him for his business," Mac said. "While he's there, they're going to try to talk to Aimee and find out if she's there of her own free will. I don't like the plan much but other than bursting in and grabbing her, I can't think of another way to get to her. I'm looking at this as reconnaissance."

"Do you think it's wise for Margo to go with him?"

"Like I said, I don't like it, but she's pretty set on doing this."

"I'm not surprised. Well, keep me posted and please tell Margo—them—to be careful. Tell them the Gordons are planning to leave for Bangkok tomorrow. I asked them to get in touch with you as soon as they get to their hotel. Thanks for all you're doing. I wish I could be there to help. And, Mac, please look after Margo."

Sam hung up the phone and leaned back in his office chair. He hated this feeling of helplessness. He wanted to be the one to solve this case, nail that bastard Huron, and bring Aimee home safely for Margo.

CHAPTER 33

RICK

Rick made sure his cargo manager understood his desire to attend Mano Huron's party was more than a business call. He gave his cargo manager the impression the loss of his wife and the strain of her long illness had left a void in his life—a void a meaningless encounter might fill for a short time. For that reason, he had decided not to bring Margo. Entering the hotel dining room, he felt the same rush he felt the first time he saw her at the Christmas party all those years ago. Although she was an older version of that girl, she was still beautiful. She waved at him from a table along the windows. One shapely leg peeked through the side slit in her floral sundress. He sucked in his breath remembering her legs wrapped around him when they made love. *Get a grip, old man. She's not going to like what you're going to tell her; let alone be interested in travelling down memory lane right now.*

"Hi, Kitt. You look great. I just got off the phone with Huron's office," Rick said, not wanting to delay the bad news. "I got the invitation to the party, but they asked that I not bring you. They said it will be businessmen only."

"What? Did you tell them I was your assistant and you needed me to come along?" Margo said, struggling to keep her voice down. "I have to see Aimee and see that she's okay."

"I know, dear, but I didn't want to blow the chance at getting to at least talk with her, and I don't want to arouse any suspicion about my motives."

"Well, what am I supposed to do in the meantime? It'll drive me crazy not knowing what's going on," Margo said, twisting her napkin.

"Let's ask Mac if you can ride along with him on surveillance," Rick offered. "He'll be here shortly to brief us on any new information and instruct me on what I need to do at the party. Believe me, I would be much happier if you were with me, but we have to focus on helping Aimee."

Mac waved to Rick from the dining room entrance and strode toward their table.

"I believe I have some good news for you. My friend in the Thai police says an undercover operation is gathering evidence on Huron's drug and trafficking business. They're getting close to an arrest and Pim Sakda is part of that effort. It seems she believes Huron was responsible for the abduction and death of her cousin and wanted to help take him down. She went to work in Huron's company to assist the police in collecting evidence."

"So, maybe she can help us get Aimee out before she's harmed," Margo said hopefully.

"Well, yes, but it's tricky," Mac said. "We don't want to do anything to jeopardize the operation and her life or Aimee's."

"Of course," Margo agreed.

"I secured an invitation to the party tonight, Mac," Rick interjected, "but the stipulation is that I not bring Margo with me as it will be businessmen only. So, how do you want me to proceed?"

"That's even better. No offense, Margo, I wasn't happy about putting the two of you at risk. This will give Rick an opportunity to make Huron think he's interested in his girls entertaining him, especially Pim. Rick, you need to meet her, let her know who you are, and that you want to help her get Aimee out of there."

"Mac, I can't just sit around the hotel wondering what's happening. Can I come with you on the stakeout? I promise I won't get in your way or cause any trouble," Margo pleaded.

"Okay, but you have to listen to me and follow my instructions," Mac said reluctantly. "Actually, it might help. If they spot my car, they'll see that I'm just entertaining a pretty woman. You ready to be my girl for the night?" Mac quipped.

"I can do that," Margo said, attempting a smile.

"Rick, you must be very careful when you talk with Pim. Be aware of your surroundings. Stay clear of anything that looks like it could house a camera or microphone. Huron wants to know everything that goes on in his house. Play the part of an admirer until you can get her to an open area. She'll help you. Be sure no one is standing near enough to hear what you're saying to her. The good thing is that it'll seem natural if you're interested in her for you to whisper in her ear. Since she's working undercover, she'll have a listening device on her. She'll also want to be sure no one is listening except her team. What time are you supposed to be there?"

"The party starts at nine tonight. My cargo manager will take me there and introduce me to Huron. I made sure he knew I didn't want him hanging around. I told him I'd call a car to bring me back to the hotel. He thinks I'm just looking for a little female companionship," Rick said, glancing sideways at Margo.

"That's good," Mac said. "When you speak with Pim, say Sud told you about her mission. Sud is with the Thai P.D. He's leading the investigation into Huron. Let her know you're there to help her and you want to know what you can do. I think it would be okay if you ask her to introduce you to Aimee. Huron must believe it's because you're attracted to her."

"Oh my God, that sounds horrible," Margo exclaimed. "He's her father!"

"I know, I know, but that's what we're dealing with. Human Trafficking, sex trafficking, is big business. To Huron, it's a matter of supply and demand; he wants to be sure he has a good product. I hate to be so blunt, but if we're going to help Aimee, you need to understand that no matter how repulsive it is to us, she and the other girls are just commodities to him."

Margo swallowed the lump in her throat and resisted the tears welling up in her eyes. "I understand, but I don't have to like it."

Rick reached over and patted her hand. "Don't worry. I'll look out for our little girl."

"Margo, I'll pick you up here at one-thirty to go to the airport. We'll take the three-thirty flight to Phuket," Mac said. "I'm booked at the Holiday Inn there. I'll make a reservation for you too. Rick, I assume your cargo manager has taken care of your flight and hotel."

"Yes, he'll accompany me there. I'll tell him he can return to Bangkok after he drops me off at the villa. Don't want him to get involved in what we're up to."

"As soon as you check in, call the second number on my card. That's my partner's number at our office in Phuket. Give him your hotel and room number and the time you're being picked up. We aren't going to be able to park within sight of the villa as it's on a hillside. We'll be down the hill and will know when you arrive and leave."

CHAPTER 34

PIM

"Come in, come in," Mano Huron motioned to Pim from behind his desk. "I need to talk with you. Apparently, Miss Gordon went exploring last night and ended up in the corridor to the girls' bedrooms. My man sent her back to her room, but you can't let that happen again," Mano said, fixing his dark eyes on Pim.

"No, sir," Pim said. "I thought she was down for the night."

"About the party tonight, I need you to ensure that any of my guests who approach Miss Gordon are made aware that she is just our American guest and not available for their pleasure. Do you understand?"

"Yes sir. I'll be sure to look after her."

Pim was relieved that Huron was moving slowly with Aimee. She might be able to get her out before any harm came to her.

"Good," Mano said, his lips curling. "When she finds out that Kris has abandoned her, I'll make sure she understands that I am the one protecting her from harm. She'll soon come to appreciate the lifestyle and comfort I can offer her."

It wasn't the first time Pim had noticed the shift in Mano's dark eyes from charmer to predator. *So, he wants Aimee for himself or at least he will be the one to 'break her in'.* Pim hoped he didn't notice the shudder that passed through her body as she rose from the chair.

"She is fortunate to have your protection," She said. *And mine too,* she thought as she exited the room.

"Pim," Huron called out, "this evening before the guests arrive, bring Miss Gordon to me here."

"Yes, Mano," she nodded and closed his office door. *What is he planning to do with Aimee? I hope Sud is moving quickly.*

When Pim went to work for Mano Huron, she was confident in her resume and immediately set about becoming an invaluable asset to his silk business. Whenever he invited her to his home in Phuket, she made it a point to stay away from the corridor that led to the girls' rooms. She pleased him by assuming the role of a hostess for his clients. Pim had heard the Thai phrase "treat to food, lay down the mat" referring to the practice of welcoming high-ranking officials and clients with the finest food and drink and then bringing out young girls, often referred to as "dessert," to provide sex services. She had somehow justified it partly because she had grown up around it and partly because she believed the women were at least being taken care of. Unfortunately, girls, especially poor girls, were viewed as subordinate to men. She began quietly gathering information from the girls who came to the villa to find out if they were willing participants in Huron's "escort service." She discovered they had been taken from their homes and families and brought to Bangkok from various parts of Asia and Africa on the promise of a well-paying job in Huron's factory. Pim knew about the dark underbelly of Thailand and the sex trade but before her cousin was taken, she had always thought that only girls with no family were involved. When Sunisa was caught up in it and lost her life, Pim understood it was a sinister form of slavery. A few times, a girl would confide in her that she was frightened, but then that girl would suddenly disappear from the villa. Each time, Pim had reported it to Sud, hoping he could find them. She didn't have the courage to ask Sud about them or she wouldn't be able to hide her disgust and anger from Huron. It was difficult enough to push Sunisa out of her thoughts every time she spoke to him.

Pim knew Aimee trusted her so she decided she needed to keep Aimee away from the other girls as much as possible. The language barrier would serve to limit her interaction with them and encourage her dependence on Pim until they could get her to safety.

Pim found Aimee lounging by the pool, looking fresh and youthful in a yellow-and-white floral bathing suit. A floppy straw hat shaded her eyes as she half-dozed on a blue-striped chaise.

"There you are," Pim said, interrupting her reverie. "I thought we could decide what you want to wear for the party tonight."

"Can we wait until Kris gets here?"

"I'm sorry, Aimee. Kris just phoned to say he's been held up with business and won't be here tonight."

"What?" Aimee sat straight up on the chaise and pushed the brim of her hat back to see Pim. "He promised he'd be here tonight. I don't understand. Can we go back to Bangkok so I can see him when he gets through work? I need to convince him to let my parents come to the wedding." She rushed on. "I've been thinking that since there's a civil ceremony first and we'll already be married in the eyes of the law, my parents won't be able to stop us. Oh, Pim, I really want them at my wedding. I want my father to give me away. Maybe they'll even bring my best friend Debbie with them."

"I'm sorry. I know you're disappointed," Pim said soothingly. "But he has no time right now. He plans to fly over in the morning. You can talk to him about it then. Now, let's pick out something beautiful for tonight."

After she dressed, Pim headed to Aimee's room and knocked on the door.

"Oh Aimee, you look very pretty. Come with me. Mano would like to see you before his guests arrive."

Pim led Aimee to a room next to the villa entrance. She tapped lightly on the door.

"Come in," Mano said. His voice was deep and commanding.

Pim opened the door and motioned for Aimee to proceed ahead of her.

"Ah, Miss Gordon," Mano said, rising from behind his desk, "welcome to my villa."

He walked around the desk, and taking Aimee's arm at the elbow, guided her to a sofa at the other end of the room.

"You look lovely. Please sit down," he said, and turning toward Pim, with a dismissive wave of his hand, he added, "Thank you, Pim, you can close the door."

Aimee perched on the edge of the deep blue cushions. The paneled walls and wooden plantation shutters made the room dark in comparison to the rest of the villa. Sago palms sat on either side of the windows. Torchiere lamps beside the sofa cast soft light that combined with the early evening glow from the half-opened shutters. A gold-rimmed, blue-and-white china tea set was perched on a coffee table with ornately carved legs. Mano sat down and turned to face Aimee. "Miss Gordon, may I call you Aimee? How are you enjoying my villa?" Mano went on without waiting for her response. "Would you like some tea?"

"Yes, thank you. Your villa is beautiful," she said, twisting her fingers nervously.

"I hope you're enjoying yourself." He leaned across her and picked up the teapot. "What do you take in your tea?" His breath smelled sweet and felt warm on her cheek.

"Just plain, thank you," she said, moving slightly away.

"I understand Kris had to stay in Bangkok for some business. Don't worry. I'll make sure you enjoy yourself. Tell me, do you think you're going to like living in Thailand?"

"Yes, I do love it here."

"I understand you two plan to marry. Have you discussed when and where?"

"Not yet. I was hoping we could talk about it tonight."

He leaned in and took her hands in his.

"What would you think about being married here at the villa?"

"Really? That would be wonderful," she said, her eyes widening.

"Then we'll have to make that happen," he said, releasing her hands and leaning back.

Her excitement made her want to hug Mano, but something made her pull back. "Thank you so much," she said, awkwardly reaching for her tea.

"Aimee, I promise you can have a wonderful life here." Mano looked at his watch, stood, and held out his hand. "Come, I believe the party is about to start."

CHAPTER 35

RICK

Rick's cargo manager talked nonstop on the plane from Bangkok. They took a brief tour of the operation in Phuket. Rick tried to look duly impressed all the while thinking about what might transpire at the villa. He was anxious to see Aimee in person. It still hadn't really sunk in that he had a child--not really a child but a teenager. He wondered again if he would be able to be a part of her life and of Margo's when this was all over. It was all so surreal.

Phuket's lush, tropical climate and pristine white sand beaches made it easy to understand its appeal to the wealthy of Thailand as well as tourists. As their car climbed the hill toward the villa, the full moon lit the sea below, turning it from azure to sapphire. It was difficult for Rick to fathom that this lovely place could harbor the horrendous business of sex trafficking. Or more accurately, sex trafficking was what afforded Huron this lavish lifestyle. It was sickening.

They pulled up to the entrance of the villa and were greeted by two young men. One of the young men escorted them to the open front door while the other slid into the driver's side and sped off to park the car. Mano Huron stood at the entrance looking very distinguished in white linen slacks and an iridescent purple, short-sleeved silk shirt with a mandarin collar. Removing their shoes, Rick noted that Huron was taller than most of the Thai men he had seen.

"I am Ned Leekpai, the cargo manager in Bangkok and this is Rick Cathcart, our senior vice president, sir," he said, half bowing toward Huron. "We thank you for inviting us."

"Welcome to my home," Mano said, extending his hand to Rick.

"It's a pleasure to meet you, Mr. Huron," Rick said, grasping his hand.

"Please, call me Mano."

"And call me Rick."

"Please come in," Mano said as he gestured toward the expansive, living room filled with small groups of middle-aged men surrounded by young girls dressed in traditional one-shoulder tops that stopped at their midriff and long, tight skirts in bright jewel colors with slits up one side. Silk scarves embellished with embroidery matching the borders of the hems of the skirts hung over one shoulder and crossed diagonally over their hips. The girls were of every size, skin color, and ethnicity, and they had one thing in common, they were all lovely.

"What will you have to drink?"

"Your choice, Mano," Rick said. "This is my first time here so I'm enjoying the local food and drink."

Huron motioned to one of the waiters carrying a tray of drinks. "Please try our Sangsom. Although it is often referred to as a whiskey, it's brewed from sugarcane so it is categorized as rum."

"I'm happy to have the chance to thank you in person for all of the cargo business your company gives us," Rick said, selecting a drink from the tray. "If there is ever anything we, I, can do for you, please let me know."

"Thank you. I'll do that. Now, let me introduce you to some of my guests, who I am sure, are also clients of yours."

Rick scanned the room looking for Aimee. When he spotted her in a far corner of the living room, his heart skipped a beat. She was a younger version of Margo. She was seated on a loveseat, engrossed in a conversation with an attractive Thai woman. Aimee's head was lowered toward the woman. The woman's arm was around Aimee's shoulder. Mano steered both men around the room introducing them to various businessmen who rose and shook hands while looking slightly annoyed that their conversations with the young ladies were interrupted.

"Who's that woman over there?" Rick asked, nodding his head toward Pim. "I'm interested in meeting her."

"Certainly, she's Pim Sakda, my marketing manager," Mano replied.

Huron motioned for Pim to join them. She stood, bent over to pat Aimee on the shoulder, and crossed the room to Mano.

"Pim, this is Mr. Cathcart. His airline handles our cargo business."

"A pleasure to meet you," Rick said bowing slightly. "Would you like a drink? You can tell me what I can do to ensure we're handling your business in the best way possible."

"Yes, go ahead, my dear," Mano said.

"This is quite a place," Rick said, taking a drink from a waiter's out-stretched tray and handing it to Pim. "Would you mind showing me the terrace? It looks like there's a great view."

They stepped through the open terrace doors. A couple in the far corner moved further into the shadows. The full moon glinted on lapping waves and strips of white sand. Below, soft lights shone through the water of the tiled pool. Floodlights at the base of palm trees cast feathery shapes on the cabanas surrounding the pool.

"Beautiful view," Rick said leaning toward Pim's ear. "Sud told me about your assignment," he whispered. "I'm a friend of Aimee Gordon's parents. I'm here to help in any way I can. I won't get in your way or cause trouble. I just need to ensure she's okay."

Pim gave a lilting laugh to ensure that anyone watching would believe Rick was whispering sweet nothings in her ear. She tilted her head and whispered in his ear. "She's fine, but I hope to have her out of here by tomorrow. Huron wants her for himself and I don't intend to let that happen. We'd better go back in before he gets suspicious. In the meantime, I need to introduce you to some of the other girls."

Aimee hurried across the room just as Rick and Pim were coming in from the terrace. "I was wondering where you went."

"Mr. Cathcart, this is Aimee Gordon," Pim said. "She's a recent transplant from America and is engaged to a friend of mine here."

"Good to meet you, Miss Gordon," Rick said resisting the urge to hug her. "Where are you from in the States?"

"Ventura, California," Aimee replied.

"I know it well. Nice area. Do you plan to return there or are you and your husband going to live in Thailand?"

"We plan to live here. It will definitely be a change, but I think the country and people are lovely. My fiancé, Kris, is going to make sure I'm happy here. I already have Pim as my first girlfriend," she said, glancing sweetly at Pim.

Rick thought Aimee's cheerfulness seemed a little forced. He was certain she had no clue about the danger she was in. He wanted to grab her and run. He was glad she seemed to trust Pim and that Pim was there to protect her.

Rick was also aware of Mano Huron watching them from across the room.

"Well, come Mr. Cathcart, let me introduce you to some of the other ladies. I'll be right back, Aimee."

"Nice meeting you, Miss Gordon. I hope you'll be very happy in your new home."

As Pim guided Rick toward a young girl with copper-colored skin and dressed in a dark green sari, she leaned in and whispered, "I will communicate with you through Sud. He'll let you know how we can use your help. Thank you."

"I'll be heading out, Mr. Cathcart," Ned said approaching Rick and Pim.

Suddenly, Rick felt the urge to get out of there. Seeing Aimee here in Huron's clutches made him sick to his stomach.

"Hang on, Ned. I'm not feeling too well. Must be something I ate," he said. "I'll go with you. Let me say goodbye to Mr. Huron."

He excused himself from Pim and headed across the room to Mano Huron.

"I'm so sorry, Mano, but I'm afraid I have to cut the night short. I'm not feeling too well. Anyway, I really appreciate being invited to your beautiful home," Rick said, extending his hand. "I plan to be here a few more days. I hope I can come back before I have to return to the States."

"You are always welcome. Just give my office a call."

"I will and thanks again. It was good meeting you. Remember, anything we can do for you, just call," Rick said, handing Mano his business card.

Mac and Margo watched Ned's car return down the hill with Rick in the passenger seat.

"I wonder what happened. I hope Huron isn't on to Rick," Mac said.

He pulled away from the curb and followed at a safe distance. Ned dropped Rick off at his hotel.

"I'll be heading back to Bangkok unless you need me to stay."

"No thanks, Ned. I think I'll stay another day in Phuket. I could use some time to relax and do some sightseeing."

"I understand, sir, just call my office if you need anything."

As soon as Ned pulled away, Rick headed for the bar to wait for Mac and Margo to arrive.

"What happened? Did you see her?" Margo asked anxiously.

"I did and it was like looking at you eighteen years ago. She's lovely."

Margo's cheeks turned pink.

"Did you talk to her?" Mac asked. "Did you talk to Pim?"

"Yes, I did both. I had Pim take me out on the terrace. As instructed, I whispered in her ear and told her I was a friend of Aimee's parents who just wanted to know if she was okay. She said Huron wants Aimee for himself; she's hoping to get her out of there tomorrow. She didn't tell me the plan but said she would be in touch through Sud."

"He wants her for himself? Oh my God, Rick," Margo covered her mouth with both hands. Rick put his arm around her shoulder and squeezed. "What about Aimee? Is she all right? What did she say?"

"Frankly, I got the feeling she doesn't have a clue what's going on over there. She said her fiancé promised to take care of her and that she thinks she'll like living here. If she was having any misgivings, she was doing a good job of hiding it. At least she trusts Pim. The thought of her there with the other girls made me sick. I just couldn't stay. I was afraid Huron might sense my disgust."

"Every time I think about those poor girls and the fact that Aimee is in such danger, I want to throw up. When this is all over, Rick, we have to find a way to bring awareness about human trafficking. I've been to Bangkok many times to visit my friends, but I never thought about it and there was never any discussion with them. I guess I just thought it was something that affected people over here; certainly, not something that would reach into my life."

"The government isn't motivated to go after these guys because it's part of the tourism industry and brings in a lot of money. Not to mention the fact that most of the authorities are getting their fair share of payoffs to leave them alone," Mac interjected. "And, as you both now know, it's not just here anymore. They're expanding into the States. You need to get an invitation to Huron's tomorrow night. Sud tells me they have enough evidence on Huron's business, including the trafficking, to make the raid and arrest him."

"I'm sure I can. What do they want me to do?"

"Help Pim get Aimee out before the raid. Just follow her instructions."

"Won't that be dangerous?" Margo interrupted.

"Sud has someone on the inside besides Pim. He'll help you get her out of the villa and down the hill where Margo and I will be waiting," Mac explained. "The trick's going to be for you to get Aimee to trust you. Pim will help with that. Are you sure you can do this?"

"I have to do it," Rick squeezed Margo's hand. "That's what we came here for."

"Let me know when you've secured the invitation. "Once that's done, I'll see how Sud wants us to proceed."

CHAPTER 36

PIM

In her room, Pim slipped into the bathroom and turning her back to the camera, dropped her robe, and stepped into the shower. As the warm water rushed over her, she lifted the pendant to her mouth. "Sud, I made contact with the American. I hope the raid is going to be soon. I'm not sure how much longer it will be before Huron has his way with Aimee."

She held the pendant to her ear. "The new gardener is one of my men. Meet him by the plumeria bushes at nine in the morning. He'll tell you the plan. I can say it will be tomorrow night. Take care of yourself and be careful."

Pim awoke with a start when her alarm went off. She threw on her bathing suit and cover-up. Pushing her feet into her flip-flops, she headed down the hall to the kitchen. The house was quiet. A servant greeted her in Thai and poured her an iced coffee. She carried it to the terrace. The sweet, cold drink refreshed her as she inhaled the sea breeze. Spotting the gardener clipping hedges below, her heart lurched. She raised her glass in a small salute. *Today is for you, Sunisa.*

When she returned from the balcony, the remnants of last night's party were being removed and two young men were sweeping the floors and polishing the tables.

"Where is Mr. Huron?" Pim inquired of one of them.

"He has gone to his office in Bangkok. He will be back for the party tonight," the young man answered in Thai.

"I'll be at the pool if Miss Gordon is looking for me," Pim said over her shoulder as she descended the steps to the first level walkout.

She chose a chaise out of sight of the balcony and laid a towel across it. Glancing around, she spotted the gardener behind the plumeria bushes. Carrying her iced coffee, she strolled over to one of the bushes and caressed a flower.

"The raid is planned for eleven tonight," the gardener said in a low voice from behind the plumeria bush. "We want to be sure the party is in full swing and that we're able to arrest some of the men in the girls' rooms. Mr. Cathcart will be at the party and is ready to help you. At ten-forty-five, you are to bring Miss Gordon to the lower-level bathroom by the pool. There will be a change of clothes for her in the hamper inside the door."

"What should I tell her to get her to come with me?"

"Tell her you believe something has happened to Montri and that Mr. Huron has something to do with him not coming back," the gardener said.

"That should work. She's been asking about Kris. If he doesn't show up tonight, she'll believe something's wrong. But how is Mr. Cathcart going to help me?"

"He's been instructed to meet both of you at the bathroom. Tell Miss Gordon he's going to get her out of there and back to Kris. He'll take her through the garden where one of our men will meet them and guide them down the hill to a waiting car. For your safety and to give them time to get away, you must go back to the party. As soon as they're safely out, we'll commence the raid. My men know who you are. They'll arrest you so as not to arouse suspicion. Sud wanted me to be sure you're okay with all of this."

"Yes, I'll be fine," Pim said, strolling along the hedge pretending to inspect each bloom. "I'd better get back to the pool. By the way, Huron is in Bangkok right now, but plans to be back for the party tonight."

"Yes, we know. We're hoping he hasn't been tipped off. We have a man on him."

"Pim, Pim," Aimee called from the balcony. "What are you doing?"

"Come down and sit with me. The sun feels so good," Pim said, returning to her chaise.

Aimee bounced down the steps to the pool level, carrying her floppy hat and beach towel. She plopped down on a chaise next to Pim.

"I can't wait for Kris to get here. It seems like forever since I've seen him."

Aimee's exuberance reminded Pim of how young and innocent she was.

"I'm sure he'll be here by tonight. There's another party so you'll want to find something very special to wear. Now, put on some sunscreen so you don't meet him looking like a lobster," Pim laughed.

CHAPTER 37

RICK

Rick and Margo sat across from Mac in the hotel bar.

"I've secured the invitation to the party tonight," Rick said. "What am I supposed to do?"

"The raid is set for eleven," Mac answered. "Pim will get Aimee down to the bathroom on the lower level by the pool at ten forty-five. She'll have her change her clothes. You'll meet them there. Pim will tell Aimee Kris is in trouble and that you're going to take her to him. You and Aimee will go through the garden where you'll be met by one of Sud's men who will guide you down the hill to Margo and me. Then the raid will commence."

"How am I going to get down to the pool without Huron becoming suspicious?" Rick asked, as the danger of it all began to sink in.

"Pim will select a girl to entertain you. You are to ask her to go down to the pool with you. Then you'll send her back to the party to get you another drink. Since the girls have been groomed to meet all your needs, she'll do as you ask. After you and Aimee escape, Pim will go back to the party and delay the girl from going back to the pool. By the time you get Aimee down the hill to us, the raid will have already begun."

"Oh, Rick, I'm so scared for you and Aimee," Margo said.

"I'll be okay, Kitt. You forget I was in the military before I went to work for the company. A guy doesn't forget his training. Besides, it's for Aimee,"

Rick said, grateful Margo couldn't hear his racing heartbeat. He wiped his sweaty palms on his napkin and reached over to squeeze her hand.

When the taxi dropped Rick off at the villa at nine-thirty, the afternoon conversation was running through his head on a loop. *Don't get distracted. You can do this. Our child is in danger. Margo's depending on you.*

Rick was greeted at the door and ushered in by a Thai servant. The living room looked much the same as it had the night before with the exception of a new group of men in intimate poses and in conversation with the girls. Once again, he felt sick to his stomach as he thought about what these men were doing to these young girls. Now he was going to have to act like one of them. He scanned the room and spotted Mano Huron surrounded by a few of his "clients". Rick hated that term being applied to his obscene business.

"Ah, Mr. Cathcart, I'm glad you decided to come back," said Mano, approaching him with an outstretched hand. "It was a shame you couldn't stay last night."

"Please call me Rick. Yes, I don't know what I ate, but I was up half the night. I'm better now and looking forward to enjoying myself."

Huron gave a knowing chuckle. "Well, you can have some fun tonight. Let's start you off with a drink."

Pim and Aimee sat in a chair by the balcony door.

"Pim," Mano called. "Mr. Cathcart has arrived. Please come and introduce him to the other guests."

Pim rose and patting Aimee on the back, headed toward Mano.

"Pim, you remember Mr. Cathcart?"

"Of course, Mr. Cathcart, how nice to see you again," Pim said, bowing slightly.

"Pim will introduce you to some of the ladies, and please, have something to eat."

Pim escorted Rick to the buffet table.

"The girl I have chosen for you is Meesang," she said. "I have told her you are a recent widower and not to expect you to be like the other men; that she must take it slow."

Rick jerked his head sideways to look at Pim. "How do you know about my wife?"

"Our mutual friend does his homework. Anyway, it will help us carry out our mission," she whispered.

Meesang was sweet and shy. She spoke some English and inquired about his life in America. Rick tried not to check his watch. Time was moving way too slowly for him. At one point, he led Meesang over to Aimee. He was keenly aware that Huron was watching him.

"Hello again," Rick said cheerfully. "How are you enjoying your time in Phuket?"

"Fine but I'm anxious to see my fiancé. He should be here any minute."

"Wonderful. How are the plans for the wedding coming?"

"Pim has been helping me, but for the most part, we're only looking at magazines. I hope to be back in Bangkok by tomorrow so I can look for a dress. We might decide to get married here. Mr. Huron has been kind enough to offer the use of his villa for the wedding."

Rick was having a hard time concealing his anger at Huron and his disbelief that Aimee could be so taken in by him and this Kris guy. But then he reminded himself of her youth and privileged life. His paternal instinct was to grab her and make a run for it, but he knew that was a foolish notion. Instead, he heard himself saying, "This would be a beautiful place to have a wedding. Have a nice evening."

Rick put his arm around Meesang's waist and took her to one of the loveseats. "Tell me about Thailand."

"Pim, where's Kris?" Aimee said. "I don't understand why he isn't here yet."

"Let's get some air. The beach looks beautiful in the moonlight. I'm sure Kris will be here soon."

Pim approached Mano.

"Mano, I'm going to take Aimee down to the beach. She's upset that Kris isn't here and I need to try to calm her down."

"Fine, but don't be gone long," he said, his eyes narrowing. "We need to tell her tonight that he's not coming back, but I don't want to do it until my guests are settled in their rooms."

Pim returned to Aimee and guided her toward the open doors to the terrace.

Rick rose and turned to Meesang. "Why don't we go down to the pool? It's a lovely evening."

Pim and Aimee descended the stairs to the pool level. Arriving at the bathroom door, she pushed Aimee in.

"What's going on? I thought we were going to the beach."

Pim grabbed Aimee's forearms tightly and fixed her eyes on hers, "Aimee, listen to me carefully. Do you trust me?"

"Yes, of course, you're my friend. What's the matter? You're scaring me."

"Aimee, something has happened to Kris. He thinks Huron had something to do with it. He sent me a message that he's in trouble with Mano and can't come to the villa."

Aimee eyes widened. She sucked in her breath. "What's happened? What kind of trouble? Is he hurt? Where is he?"

"He's not hurt, just a little roughed up. He's in a motel in Phuket. He wants you to come to him."

Pim released Aimee, reached into the hamper, and pulled out a pair of jeans and a dark, long-sleeved denim shirt. "Here, take off your dress and put these on."

Aimee shook as she struggled out of the sari and pulled on the jeans and shirt. "Where am I going? How am I going to get there? Are you coming with me?"

"I'm going to take you," Rick said, appearing at the bathroom door. "I'm Kris's friend. I know where he is. We have to leave right now before Huron misses us."

Aimee stared at Rick. "But you're the American."

"It's okay. You can trust him," Pim said. "He's here to help us. Now, I have to get back upstairs before Mano suspects something. I'll be in touch later." Pim kissed Aimee on the cheek. "Go with Mr. Cathcart. It's going to be all right."

Pim quickly ascended the stairs to the terrace and came face to face with Mano.

"Where have you been? Where's Aimee?" he asked, looking over the terrace railing.

"She's in one of the cabanas at the beach. I just came up to get her a drink. She's worried about Kris not being here. She thinks he's left her. I tried to console her, but I think a drink and a cry will calm her down."

"Where is Mr. Cathcart?

"I believe he went down to the pool with Meesang. Shall I find him?"

"Yes, I need to know if he plans to spend the rest of the evening with us."

Just then, she spotted Meesang at the terrace bar.

"Ah good, there's Meesang," she said, "Looks like she's getting a drink for Mr. Cathcart. I'll find out about his plans."

As she turned to go, Mano grabbed her arm, squeezing tightly. "As soon as my guests have gone to their rooms, bring Aimee to my office. I'll talk to her."

"Yes, Mano," Pim said, extricating her arm and heading toward Meesang.

CHAPTER 38

Rick glanced up at the balcony and spotted Mano leaning over the railing. He pushed Aimee back into the bathroom and waited. When he looked again, Mano was gone.

"Aimee, give me your hand and duck," he whispered, pulling her along the side of the house towards the garden while being careful to stay in the shadows and avoid the floodlights. Soon they were enveloped by the heavy foliage of the garden.

When they came out on the other side, a man in dark clothing and carrying a rifle stepped out of the shadows. Startled, Aimee yelped.

"It's okay. He's a friend. Come on," Rick said, keeping his voice low.

Crouching down, they crept along behind the dark figure until they reached the top of the hill. He motioned them past him. The grass was wet and slick. They slid down to the road. A black car was parked on their left. Headlights flashed on and off. Rick pushed Aimee toward Mac's car, grabbed the handle, and pulled the back door open for her to slide in.

Catching his breath, he leaned into the back. "These are my friends, Aimee. This is Margo and that's Mac. We're going to take good care of you." He jumped into the front seat beside Mac.

"Where's Kris. Is he okay?"

The sound of shouting and gunfire emanated from the top of the hill at the villa.

"What's that noise? What's going on?" She turned towards Margo, her eyes filled with fear.

"It's the police. Aimee, Mano Huron is a very bad man. The police have been investigating him for a long time. He's keeping the young women in the villa captive and he intended that for you," Margo said, reaching for her hand.

Aimee jerked her hand away and began to shake. She leaned forward towards Rick in the front seat. "I don't understand. I thought you were taking me to Kris. Pim said he's hurt. I need to see him."

"We'll explain it all to you later. Right now, we need to get out of here," Rick said. "Let's go Mac."

Aimee slumped back in the seat and hugged herself.

Mac switched the headlights on and sped off. Police cars raced past them, lights flashing, sirens screaming.

Inside the villa, the sound of clinking glasses and soft giggles turned to screams and the slap of bare feet running on the teak floors. Dark-clothed men in riot gear sprang from the terrace, through the open glass doors, pointing rifles and shouting "down on the floor" in Thai. Flanked by his two bodyguards, Huron raced toward the entrance only to be met by the Royal Thai police.

"What's the meaning of this?" he shouted in Thai.

"We have a warrant for your arrest on human trafficking charges," Sud responded, as one of the officers came up behind Mano and handcuffed him. "You too, Miss Sakda" he said, pointing at Pim.

An officer stepped up behind her and handcuffed her.

Other officers shoved Huron's two bodyguards and the male servants face down on the floor and quickly handcuffed them.

Pim wriggled her body and protested in Thai.

The policemen raced down the corridor, kicking the doors open, rifles pointed, shouting "come out with your hands up" in Thai. Half-clothed men emerging from the rooms sputtering obscenities were herded into the living room. They were followed by frightened, whimpering young girls clutching their robes about their naked bodies.

The girls were escorted into the living room where they joined others huddling together on sofas and chairs, their eyes wide with fear as their "clients" were taken out in handcuffs and loaded into one of two police wagons in front of the villa.

Sud stood in the living room. "It's all right. You're safe now. No one's going to hurt you. We're taking you to the police station to answer some questions and then you will be taken to a nice place where you will stay until we can reach your relatives. Now go quickly, get dressed and come right back here. Go, go," he commanded.

Clinging to each other, they scurried down the corridor followed by two police officers.

Outside, one of the policemen shoved Mano into the back of a police car.

"Sorry, I hope I didn't hurt you," the other policeman whispered to Pim as he pushed her into the back of another car.

They loaded the "clients," bodyguards and servants into a police wagon and the girls into another.

Sud motioned to a man in plainclothes carrying a camera. "Come with me. We need to get some shots of the rooms."

Sud and the photographer entered the open door of the first room. A four-poster bed, small chest of drawers, an end table and two upholstered chairs were the only furniture. There were no windows. Two small lamps on the dresser were draped with scarves casting a scarlet glow in the darkened room. Sud jerked the scarves off the lamps to reveal red satin sheets crumpled on the bed. Hanging from the bedposts were leather straps, handcuffs, and blindfolds. At the end of the bed lay a small, black leather whip known as a cat-o-nine tails. Two silver straws lay beside lines of white powder on one end table. Two glasses half full of a dark liquid sat on the other.

The photographer set about snapping pictures of the room and the items in it. The other rooms were the same except for the drug paraphernalia.

After a complete search of the villa, the policemen reported all was secure.

"The detectives will arrive shortly to collect evidence," Sud said to the officers he was posting at the villa. Getting into one of the vehicles, he led the caravan down the hill to the Phuket Police Station.

CHAPTER 39

AIMEE

When they arrived at the Phuket Arcadia Hotel, Aimee reached over and grabbed the car door handle. "Is this where Kris is? Is he okay?"

Rick opened the door, helped her out, put his arm around her shoulder and guided her into the hotel lobby. Margo quickly caught up with them and came around on Aimee's right side.

"Aimee, oh Aimee."

Startled at hearing her mother's voice, Aimee looked across the lobby to see her parents rushing toward her with outstretched arms. Soon she was engulfed. Helen smoothed Aimee's hair away from her face and kissed her on her forehead. "It's going to be okay, honey."

"Oh, Aimee, we're so glad you're safe. Thank you for bringing her back," Martin said, acknowledging Mac, Rick, and Margo.

"Mother, Father, what are you doing here?" Aimee asked, suddenly pulling away from their embrace. She turned toward Rick. "Where's Kris? I don't understand what's going on. I thought you were taking me to Kris."

"Aimee, we need to get out of this lobby. Please go up to your parents' room and we'll be up to tell you about Kris."

"Come on, Aimee. Let's go up to our room," Martin said, guiding her toward the elevators. "We'll explain it all to you. We're in 240," he called back over his shoulder to the others.

Helen clutched Aimee, stroking her hair. "We were so worried about you."

Martin opened the door to the suite. "Come on, let's get you cleaned up," Helen said, leading Aimee into the bathroom. Depositing her on the edge of the tub next to the sink, Helen grabbed a washcloth and held it under the warm water. She lifted Aimee's face and gently wiped the dirt and tears away.

"What's happening? Where's Kris? Why are you here?" Looking up at Helen, Aimee frowned in confusion.

She wasn't the sassy teenager who had fought with her mother over a week ago.

The girl who had run off to get married was now a frightened little child. Helen lifted her up and pressed her head to her chest, hugging her tightly.

"Aimee, Kris wasn't honest with you. He was working for Mr. Huron, who is a really bad man. Apparently, he hired Kris to take you away from us and bring you back to Bangkok. I'm so sorry, Aimee, but Kris was never going to marry you. In fact, they're probably arresting him right now. When we found out you left with him, we were frantic. We went to the police. They put us in touch with the good people who helped us get you back. I know it's a lot to take in, and it's confusing, but you must believe me, you were in grave danger."

"No, it can't be true," Aimee wailed. "He loves me. We made plans."

"Sweetheart, you've been through a lot tonight. We'll talk more in the morning, but right now, let's get you to bed."

Back in the living room, Margo and Rick sat on the sofa across from Mac and Martin. "How is she?" Margo asked, leaning forward when Helen sat down.

"Understandably, she's very shaken up and confused. I gave her a sedative. I told her the L.A. police put us in touch with you to help us when she disappeared. I said we would tell her all about it tomorrow."

"That's good. I don't think we should tell her who I am just yet," Margo said. "She's been through so much. We don't need to add to the trauma."

"I agree," Martin said. "Let Helen and I discuss it. I'll call you in the morning. Are you here in this hotel?"

"Yes, we're in suite 120," Rick responded. "I think we'd better leave so all of us can get some rest. It's been a very eventful night, but with a good ending."

"Yes, we can't thank you enough for all you've done," Helen said, giving them each a hug. "See you in the morning."

CHAPTER 40

MARGO

As they walked to the elevator, Rick put Margo's arm through his in the old, familiar way. "Kitt, stay here tonight," he whispered. "We need to talk."

Margo surprised herself when she leaned into him and nodded. It had been a very scary, stressful day and she needed to be with him tonight.

"I'll bring Margo's things from our hotel in the morning around nine. We can talk about what to tell Aimee," Mac said, holding the elevator door open at their floor.

Exiting the elevator, Margo turned toward Mac, "Thank you for everything, I, we, are so grateful."

Mac nodded as the elevator doors closed.

Back in his suite, Rick offered Margo the fluffy terry cloth robe provided by the hotel. "You'll feel better after you take a shower. You can sleep in this," he said, handing her one of his T-shirts.

Standing in the shower letting the hot water flow over her body, Margo felt the tension of the past hours begin to leave her. *We did it. We saved Aimee.*

She wiped the steam from the shower off the mirror and stood looking at herself. She felt like Rick's Margo. *My baby's father is here with me. He risked his life to save her.* A part of her felt the old yearning. *Am I ready to be with Rick in that way again? He's just lost his wife. I don't want him to confuse his grief with love for me. And then, there's Sam.* "No, you're not going to sleep with him tonight," she told the woman in the mirror.

When she came out of the bathroom, Rick hugged her tightly, kissed her on the forehead and led her into the second bedroom.

"Sleep tight, Kitt. We did it." Apparently, he had already made the decision for them both.

The ringing of the phone on the nightstand jolted Rick out of a deep sleep. He looked at his watch and was surprised to see that it was almost nine o'clock.

"Mr. Cathcart. It's Martin. Can you and Margo come to our suite in an hour? We've ordered some breakfast. Aimee's still asleep so we can discuss what and when to tell her about Margo."

Rick pulled on his pants and a T-shirt and crossed the sitting room to Margo's door. He knocked softly and was surprised when Margo opened the door fully dressed.

"Was that Martin?"

"Yes, he wants us to come to his suite in an hour. They want to talk about what to tell Aimee about who we are. Didn't you sleep well?"

"Not really. Rick, I'm so nervous. What will she think of me and what I did? That I gave her up."

"It'll be okay, Kitt. When she finds out what we went through to keep her from being hurt, she'll realize how much she means to us. In time, she'll forgive us."

"So, you're planning to tell all of them you're her birth father?"

"Yes, we're in this together. Why—don't you want me to?"

Before Margo could answer, there was a knock on the door. When he opened the door, Helen Gordon was standing there.

"I thought we were coming to your room, Helen. Please come in."

"Thank you. I need to talk with both of you about the conversation we're about to have with Aimee," Helen said, entering the room and closing the door behind her.

Margo stood behind Rick trying to push away the dread that Helen was going to ask her not to tell Aimee who she was.

"Please, come, sit down," Rick said, gesturing toward the sofa and chairs.

Helen sat on the sofa and crossed her legs at the ankles. Margo sat down on the other end of the sofa. Rick took a chair across from them.

"I told you about the incident in the doctor's office when Aimee discovered she was adopted," Helen began. "She was very angry with me. In fact, our relationship hasn't been the same since. I told her I didn't know your name or anything about you except that you weren't able to care for a baby and you did the best thing for her." Helen glanced at Margo. "I would like to tell her that it was Detective Carpenter who found you and not let her know that I gave your name to him. If she knew that I had that information and kept it from her, I don't think she'd ever be able to forgive me."

"Of course, that'll be fine," Margo said, reaching over and touching Helen's hand lightly. "But we need to tell you something as well. You see, Rick is Aimee's birth father. Oh, he didn't abandon me," Margo quickly added. "He didn't even know about Aimee until a few days ago. I guess I kinda made a mess of things by keeping it a secret from him. I was just trying to do what I thought was best at the time. I was young and not ready to be a mother or make him choose me over his wife and his career." She felt the tears well up.

Rick gave her a look of compassion.

"I'm afraid this is going to be a lot for Aimee to handle right now, especially after what she just went through," Helen said.

Margo's heart sank. She knew Helen was right, but a part of her wanted to be able to explain it all to Aimee and ask for her forgiveness. And she wanted that for Rick as well.

"It seems we all know what's best for Aimee right now," Rick interjected. "I suggest we wait until we're all back in the States on familiar ground before we tell her who we are. Mac can explain the whole Kris thing to her. I think Margo and I should stay out of the picture until we're home."

"Thank you, Rick," Helen said, relief washing over her face. "I was hoping you'd say that. After we meet with the Thai police, Martin and I are taking Aimee home tonight. When we get back, we can set up a time for us to meet at our house. Is that all right with you Margo?"

"I think that's the best thing to do." Margo felt the tension leave her body. She gave Rick a grateful look. "Please tell Martin and Aimee that we had to get back and we'll see them soon." Rick said, opening the door for Helen.

When Mac arrived at their suite with Margo's things, Rick explained the plan to him.

"I think that's wise," he said. "That girl has been through a lot and she doesn't need to be any more confused than she already is. I'll do my best to explain what was going to happen to her— hopefully, without scaring the wits out of her. Although I do want her to realize what she almost got herself into. You two did a great thing and I'm proud of all of us. The police in Singapore arrested Montri and are extraditing him back to Bangkok. Because the court deemed Huron a flight risk, they did not set bail. It looks like the Thai police did a good job of developing the case against him."

"Thanks for saving our little girl," Margo said hugging him tightly.

"Yes, Mac, don't know what we'd have done without you," Rick said, shaking his hand and clapping him on the shoulder. "Here's my card. Please send your bill to the home address I've written on the back. By the way, how is Pim? Did she get out okay?"

"Yes, they pretended to arrest her so Huron wouldn't get suspicious. They let her go this morning. I called her to let her know Aimee was safe.

CHAPTER 41

MAC

When Helen escorted Mac into their suite, Aimee and Martin were sitting at the table in the dining alcove. Aimee picked at some fruit. She lifted her head. Her eyes were puffy and red-rimmed from crying. She looked like a little girl in the big, fluffy hotel robe.

"Mr. McCallister, please come have some breakfast." Martin rose and gestured to the chair across from him. "Aimee, do you remember Mr. McCallister? He drove you back to the hotel. He's the private investigator who helped us find you."

Aimee looked up at Mac. "I guess I need to thank you, Mr. McCallister. Although I'm still confused about what happened," she said weakly.

"Please, call me Mac," he said, reaching across the table and extending his hand to Aimee. "Aimee, there are some very bad people in this world whose business it is to find young girls such as yourself and bring them to Bangkok for the purpose of selling them into slavery," Mac decided not to use the word "sex trafficking" just yet. He wanted her to hear what he had to say.

"Slavery? Oh no, you're wrong, that's not what happened to me," Aimee protested, her eyes wide. "I met Kris when I was with my parents. He worked for the bank. We've been emailing for a long time. I love him and he loves me. It must be a mistake. He'd never get mixed up in anything like that."

"I know you thought he loved you and was going to marry you, but that's how these guys work," Mac responded. "Kris Montri isn't with the bank. He works for Mano Huron. When Huron saw you in Bangkok with your parents, he hired Kris to bring you back to Bangkok. He planned to keep you for himself," Mac paused to let it sink in. "Last night, the police arrested Huron and Kris on drug and human trafficking charges. Kris was already in Singapore. He's being brought back here for trial. The girls you met at Huron's villa were being kept there against their will." Mac fixed his gaze on Aimee. "That was to be your fate as well."

Aimee shook her head in disbelief. She covered her face with her hands. "No, no, that can't be," she wailed. "We were going to get married. He was going to help me get a job with Thai Airways. We were going to travel."

Helen moved to the chair next to Aimee. "Honey, when you ran away, we were frantic. We called the police in L.A. When they found that you had left on a plane to Bangkok with Kris, they told us they had reason to believe you had been taken by these evil people. We hired Mr. McCallister to help us get you back. We just prayed it would be before something awful happened to you."

"You can thank Pim Sakda for keeping you safe," Mac interjected. "She was working undercover for the Thai Police because Mano Huron was responsible for the death of her cousin. He arranged to have her taken by a young man in the same way and she ended up dead on the beach in Phuket."

Aimee's head popped up. She stared at Mac with wide-eyed fear and sudden recognition that he was telling her the truth. "Is Pim okay?"

"Yes, she wanted me to tell you she's glad you're okay and with your parents. She wants you to know that she's still your friend."

Aimee began to tremble. Helen put her arms around her. "Oh, Mother, I'm so sorry I ran away. I was so mad at you and Father for not telling me I was adopted. I felt so alone and confused. I didn't know who I was anymore. When I told Kris about it, he was so kind and loving. He said he'd help me find my birth parents. He said he loved me. That he would be my family. He said he'd always take care of me. I can't believe I've been so foolish."

"It's all right, sweetheart. Your father and I are just so grateful that you're safe. We love you so much." She looked over at Martin and back at Aimee. "When we get home, if you still want to, we'll help you find your birth parents."

"That's right, Aimee. We'll do that," Martin responded rounding the table and kissing her on the forehead.

CHAPTER 42

MARGO

Margo sat at her kitchen table savoring the American coffee she had missed. She and Rick had come together to rescue their child. Now, they would have to explain to Aimee who they were and hope that she would forgive them.

When her phone rang, she expected to hear Rick's voice on the other end.

"Hello, Margo. It's Sam. I'm so glad you're back safe and that you were able to rescue Aimee. How are you feeling? When can I see you? I've really missed you."

"I've missed you too," Margo said, stifling a yawn. "I'm still dealing with jet lag. How about meeting for dinner?"

Margo was excited to see Sam standing outside the restaurant. Being with Rick in Bangkok had awakened her to the realization that there was a void in her heart. Until Sam kissed her on the pier, she hadn't dared to dream that anyone could love her again—not after what she'd done. When Sam flung his arms around her and hugged her tightly, she pressed her face into his chest and allowed herself to think things might change for her.

They followed the hostess to a small booth in a dark corner of the dining room. Sam kept his arm around her waist and gave her a sweet peck on her cheek as they slid in.

"I've really missed you. I was so worried for you, but Mac said you were a real trooper. How was it to finally see your daughter?"

"Sam, you can't believe how beautiful she is, but she doesn't know I'm her mother yet. We, Rick and I, decided she'd been through a lot and we should wait to drop that bombshell on her after we got back to the States. In fact, we're going to meet with her at the Gordons' tomorrow to explain everything. I'm so worried that she'll hate me for giving her up."

Sam put his arm around her shoulder. "When she realizes what you did to get her out of harm's way, I think she'll see how much you love her. And Rick, what does he want to happen?" Sam asked, hesitantly.

"Rick and I care very much for each other because we have history and Aimee, but I think we both know it won't ever be anything more than friends."

"I hope you don't mind my telling you how glad I am to hear that," he said, leaning in and kissing her deeply.

Returning the kiss, Margo felt the warmth creep up her neck and into her cheeks. "I can't promise anything, Sam, but I really missed you and want to see where this goes if you want that too."

"Are we celebrating something?" the waiter asked cheerfully.

"Yes, yes, we are," Sam said. "Bring us a bottle of your best champagne."

Margo awoke the next morning feeling both happy and anxious. Today she would tell Aimee who she was and why she had given her up for adoption. *I hope she doesn't hate me too much. She's had a good home. The home and the family that I couldn't have given her.*

The ringing phone startled her. She fumbled for it, checking the clock on her end table. "Kitt, are you up?" Rick asked. "Are you ready for the big day? I'm really nervous. What if she hates me and thinks I abandoned her?"

"I was just thinking the same thing about me. I'll make sure she knows you didn't know about her. That will help you and then she'll probably really hate me. Oh, Rick, I really did make a mess of things, didn't I?"

"Kitt, you were young. You did what you thought was right. We'll just have to make sure she understands that. I'll pick you up at eleven. What's your address?"

"No, I'll meet you at your hotel." Margo couldn't bear to have Rick see how she lived. *After this is all over, I'd better look for a better place. I can't keep putting Sam off about coming to my apartment and if I'm lucky enough to be in Aimee's life, I'll need a nice place for her to visit.* That thought brightened her and pushed the anxiety away briefly.

CHAPTER 43

AIMEE

Helen Gordon was dealing with her own anxiety. She knew that Aimee needed to be told about Margo and Rick, but she worried Aimee might blame her for not telling her sooner. She had let Aimee think she knew nothing about her birth parents. Margo and Rick had agreed to keep her secret, but she really didn't know what kind of relationship they would want in the future. They seemed like good people. They had risked their lives to help them get Aimee back. But Helen knew a mother's desire to be close to her child. She pushed those thoughts away as she prepared to welcome them into her home.

"Aimee, are you almost ready? Miss Kitteridge and Mr. Cathcart will be here shortly," she called up the stairs.

"I'll be right down, Mother."

Aimee entered the living room and leaned down to hug her father before plopping on the sofa. She fidgeted with the bottom of her T-shirt, pulling it down and smoothing it. Martin sat in his black leather recliner hiding behind the morning paper. Aimee had been told she would finally hear the whole story about her abduction and rescue and what part these people had in it.

When the doorbell rang, Helen ran her hands over her cotton floral dress, smoothing it, and touched her pearls as she went to the door. "Welcome, it's so good to see you two and be able to thank you again for all your help," she said, escorting Rick and Margo into the living room. "Aimee, you remember Mr. Cathcart and Miss Kitteridge."

Martin rose, put down the paper, and shook their hands. Aimee looked up from the sofa and nodded. "Hello."

"Please sit down," Helen said, gesturing to two easy chairs across from the sofa. "Would you like some tea?" she offered, sitting down on the sofa next to Aimee. "What do you take in it?" She poured from a white china teapot painted with tiny violets into matching teacups.

"One sugar, thank you," Margo replied.

"Just plain for me, thank you," Rick answered.

"How are you feeling, Aimee?" Margo began, trying to keep her voice steady.

"I'm okay. I still can't believe that Kris was lying to me all this time. I feel so stupid. After talking to Mr. McCallister, it's scary to think about what might have happened to me. Mother tells me I have you two to thank for saving me and I do thank you so much."

"We're just happy we could help and that it turned out well," Rick said.

"Aimee, the reason Mr. Cathcart and Miss Kitteridge got involved in helping us is why we wanted to have them come over today," Martin began. "When you ran away, we were frantic and, of course, we called the police. We told them how upset you were about finding out you were adopted. We thought you might have gone looking for your birth mother. When we told that to the police, they thought you may have found her and might be with her."

"No, no, I hadn't found out anything," Aimee protested. "I was just really upset, and Kris told me he would help me find her after we were married. I was mad at you, but I didn't try to find her."

"It's all right," Helen patted Aimee's knee. "The police did find her and," Helen took a deep breath, "Miss Kitteridge—Margo—is your birth mother."

Margo leaned forward and smiled tenderly.

"What? You're my mother?" Aimee stared at Margo and turned to look at Helen before returning her attention to Margo.

"Yes, Aimee, and, actually, I've been looking for you," Margo said quickly. "I wasn't going to try to see you. I just wanted to know you were okay. I was extremely upset when the police called me to tell me you were missing. But I was so happy to meet the wonderful people who adopted you and learn about the beautiful life you have. We found we all had a common goal of getting you back safely."

"I know this is a lot to take in, dear," Helen said, putting her arm around Aimee's shoulder. "I know you must have a lot of questions for Margo. Why don't you two go out to the porch. I'll fix us some lunch."

"Thank you, Helen. That's very kind of you." Margo said.

Aimee rose. "It's this way," she said, quickly heading toward the open French doors.

Rick and Martin sat in awkward silence.

"So, Rick, tell me about the airline business," Martin said, clearing his throat.

Helen excused herself to set out a light lunch in the dining room where, it so happened, she had a clear view of the porch.

Margo followed Aimee out. Aimee slumped down in a white-wicker chair and, crossing her arms across her chest, stared down at the tile floor. Margo perched on the front edge of the other chair. A white porcelain vase filled with sunflowers that matched the pattern on the chair cushions sat atop the round white-wicker, glass-topped table that separated them.

Leaning forward, Margo clasped her hands in her lap and cleared her throat. "First, Aimee, I want you to know you were conceived in love and giving you up was the hardest thing I've ever had to do. I wasn't much older than you when I met your father. He was my boss at the airport. I had just moved to L.A. from Seattle. He was kind to me and made me feel at home. He was very well-respected by all the employees and he cared about everyone," Margo took a deep breath and rushed on. "We didn't mean to fall in love. He was married and moving up in the company. The affair ended when he was promoted and relocated to Seattle. It wasn't until after he left that I discovered I was pregnant with you. I was scared."

"So he didn't want to marry you so you could keep me?" Aimee exclaimed, her head popping up to stare accusingly at Margo.

Margo looked down at her hands. "He didn't have a chance to make that decision. I made it for us. I didn't tell him I was pregnant. I didn't want to know if he would choose me over his wife and career. I can assure you that, in those days, we both would have lost our jobs. I know it sounds selfish and terrible, Aimee, but I wasn't ready to be a mother and certainly not ready to raise a child on my own. I took a leave of absence from work and went away to have you. I was afraid I wouldn't be able to provide for you so I agreed to the adoption." Tears welled up in Margo's eyes. She raised her head and looked deeply into Aimee's eyes. "It was the most loving thing I could think of to do for you."

"I'm eighteen. Why didn't you come looking for me sooner?" Aimee asked through clenched teeth.

"I only found out who adopted you recently. The records were sealed." Remembering her pledge to Helen and Martin, she lied, "It was only when the police called after you disappeared that I found out who your parents were. I don't expect you to forgive me for my past, but I do hope you can see how much I care about you. When I met your parents, I knew I had made the right decision for you. They love you very much and you've had a good life, haven't you?"

"Yes, but I've been very angry at them for not telling me that I was adopted. I always felt I was different from the rest of the Gordon family. I thought there was something wrong with me. Does my father know about me now?"

"Yes, but I only just told him when you went missing. At first, he was very upset with me, but the fact that you were in danger overshadowed all of that. He's a good man, Aimee. He was angry that I hadn't trusted him and hadn't told him I was pregnant, but he has forgiven me. I'm hoping you can too. Aimee, all four of your parents came together to rescue you from Kris and Huron and the life of slavery they planned for you. We all love you so much."

Aimee put her face in her hands and began to sob. "I didn't know how much danger I was in. After my mother and father told me what could have happened to me, I realized how stupid and naïve I was. It was all so romantic. I thought he was the only person who loved me. I was mad at you—whoever you were—for giving me up. I was mad at them for not telling me I was adopted. A part of me just wanted to hurt them. I guess I really messed up."

Margo stood and lifting Aimee up out of the chair, hugged her tightly. Aimee didn't hug her back, but she didn't move away.

"I know, I know," she said. "Apparently, making a mess of things is something you inherited from me." Margo leaned back and lifted Aimee's chin. "But the biggest lesson you should have learned is that you are loved by all of us."

Helen stood at the door to the porch watching Margo and Aimee cling to each other. Before she could say anything, Aimee broke from Margo's embrace and ran to Helen.

"Oh, Mama, I'm so sorry. I never meant to hurt you," she cried, hugging her tightly.

"I know, honey, and we never wanted to hurt you. We love you so much."

"Wait a minute," Aimee turned and looked back at Margo. "You said all four of my parents saved me!"

Margo approached them. The two mothers stood on either side of Aimee, entwined their arms around her waist, and took her into the living room.

"Aimee, this is Rick, your birth father," Margo said. "As you know, he came to Phuket to help rescue you."

Rick stood, crossed the room, and said, "I'm so glad you finally know who I am. May I give you a hug?"

Aimee nodded. When she looked into Rick's blue eyes, her eyes, she knew it was all true.

"Well, anyone hungry?" Helen asked, breaking the tension. Putting her arm through her husband's, she whispered. "I'll explain later."

Aimee stepped back and surveyed the four people lovingly smiling at her.

"I know I am," she said, "hungry for food and information. I need to know how you all came to Bangkok to save your daughter," she added shyly.

CHAPTER 44

MARGO

Margo and Rick sat in silence on the ride to the airport. It had been an emotionally exhausting day and now they would say goodbye for a while.

Rick broke the silence. "I'm happy that Aimee wants to stay in touch and see us once in a while. When I move back to L.A., maybe we can take her out together."

"I don't think that's such a good idea, Rick. It's a confusing situation for her as it is. If we do things with her together, I'm afraid she'll think of us as a couple. Maybe even have some ideas about the future that will affect her relationship with her parents. I want to be there for her but always with the blessing of Martin and Helen. They have given her a wonderful life. I don't want them to think we're trying to replace them."

"Of course, you're right. So, I guess that means the discussion we had in Bangkok about our relationship is settled? Just friends?"

"I think that's best for both of us. Rick, I will always love you but I'm not 'in love' with you. As much as you might think differently right now, you're not in love with me. You still have grieving to do over the loss of Carol. What we had was bound to burn itself out, but we're lucky to have Aimee because of it."

"Thank you for that, Kitt. I'm a father and that's something I never thought I'd be able to say."

Margo leaned over and kissed him on the cheek. "You're welcome."

That evening, Margo and Sam met at the California Pizza Kitchen again.

"It went better than I expected," Margo said, hugging Sam. "Aimee wants to stay in touch with both Rick and me. Martin and Helen support her in that desire. They are really great people. I can tell how much they love her. I'm eternally grateful that they were the ones who adopted her. When Rick found out she wants to work for the airlines instead of going to college, he told the Gordons he would like to help her with that if they'll let him. I could tell they were more comfortable with the idea if Rick and I would be watching over her. I can't believe how wonderful they've been to us."

"Us? So you and Rick are going to do things together with Aimee? As a couple?"

Margo put her hand on his. "No, we've agreed; we're just friends. There's no future for us as a couple. We're just happy to have found Aimee, which by the way, wouldn't have happened without you," Margo said, leaning over and kissing him. "Don't worry. I only have room in my heart for one man. Hopefully, that man is going to take me for a walk on the pier after our pizza."

"You can count on it."

Four Years Later

AIMEE

With the help of Rick and Margo, Aimee became a flight attendant for their airline. She is actively involved in a training program established by the company for flight attendants. It teaches them how to spot possible cases of human trafficking. Telling her story and knowing that she may be preventing some other girl from going through such an ordeal has helped her heal. Although it's hard to quantify, authorities have credited the program with helping them identify and arrest many of those involved in this horrendous business.

For more information, see *Business Insider,* Mark Matousek, February 13, 2020, "Delta and United flight attendants reveal how they spot victims of human trafficking."

MANO and KRIS

Mano Huron was convicted of drug trafficking and human trafficking and is incarcerated for life in the Bang Kwang Central Prison in Nonthaburi Province, Thailand.

Kris Montri was convicted of aiding and abetting human trafficking and is incarcerated in the same facility.

MARGO, RICK and SAM

Margo is no longer the "bag lady" or "Margurite," but the Margo who is happily married to Detective Sam Carpenter.

Rick Cathcart is now the president of the airline and just announced his engagement to the manager of corporate affairs.

THE GORDONS

Martin and Helen enjoy flying with Aimee on one of her routes and bragging to the other passengers about their wonderful daughter.

EPILOGUE

Aimee's story takes place in early 1998. Following is information on Human Trafficking in Thailand and the United States in the 1990s and currently.

Sex Trafficking in Thailand in the 1990s

According to Wikipedia, "Sex trafficking in Thailand is human trafficking for the purpose of sexual exploitation and slavery that occurs in the Kingdom of Thailand. Thailand is a country of origin, destination, and transit for sex trafficking. It is estimated that during the 1990s the number of people engaged in the sex industry in Thailand was no fewer than 400,000. Thailand's sex industry is worth over 6.4 billion dollars, having roughly 3 to 5 million regular customers."

Sex Trafficking in Thailand in 2019

Although Thailand has established laws over the years to mitigate human trafficking, the 2019 Trafficking In Persons Report published by the U. S. State Department classified them as Tier 2, and states: "The Government of Thailand does not fully meet the minimum standards for the elimination of trafficking, but is making significant efforts to do so."

Sex Trafficking in the United States in the 1990s

According to U.S. State Department Archives, "President Clinton issued a directive on March 11, 1998, establishing the United States' strategy to combat the trafficking of persons around the world. The strategy involves prevention, protection, and assistance for trafficking victims, and prosecution of and enforcement against traffickers. The United States views trafficking as a global problem that must be addressed through country-specific, anti-trafficking initiatives as well as by regional cooperation."

Sex Trafficking in the United States in 2020

The 2020 Trafficking In Persons Report published by the U. S. State Department classified the United States of America as Tier 1, and states: "The Government of the United States fully meets the minimum standards for the elimination of trafficking. The government continued to demonstrate serious and sustained efforts during the reporting period; therefore the United States remained on Tier 1. These efforts included increasing the number of investigations, increasing the amount of funding for victim services, and increasing enforcement of the prohibition of imports made wholly or in part by forced labor. Although the government meets the minimum standards, it prosecuted fewer cases and secured convictions against fewer traffickers, issued fewer victims trafficking-specific immigration benefits, and did not adequately screen vulnerable populations for human trafficking indicators."

Human Trafficking in Phoenix Arizona

For more information on the human trafficking recovery program at the Phoenix Dream Center, go to their website: phoenixdreamcenter.org.

For the national anti-trafficking hotline and resource center serving victims, survivors, and the anti-trafficking community.
Call 1-888-373-7888 (TTY: 711) Text 233733. Use the online Live Chat.

ACKNOWLEDGEMENTS

I have always believed that the right people come into our lives at exactly the right time.

After losing my dear mother who had been with me for fourteen years, I found myself thinking about the next chapter of my life. I'd always wondered if I could write. My friends often told me I was a good storyteller but my busy career left me no time to pursue writing. Enter Susan Pohlman, my teacher, encourager, editor, and friend. I'll always remember what Susan told us in the first class I took on memoir in 2013. She said that, after taking the class, we would never read a book or watch a movie in the same way again. Boy, was she right! Susan introduced me to a whole new world of creativity, craft, and most importantly, a tribe of authors who have kept me laughing, energized, supported, and dare I say, younger than my years. So thank you, Susan.

A special thank you to my beta readers Jennifer Clark, Trish Dolasinski, Sue Hayes, Cindy Knudsen, Linda McGuire, and Carolyn Placzek who gave generously of their time, expertise and wisdom. Your feedback made for a better product.

My research was aided by the gracious assistance of Detective Scott Carpenter, former member of the Special Victims Unit of the Scottsdale AZ Police Department and Joe Gordon, Supervisory Special Agent (retired), US Bureau of Alcohol, Tobacco & Firearms (ATF).

Thank you to Dr. Robert Desman who has always encouraged and supported me and made it possible for this book to come to fruition.

My family and friends have been my cheerleaders all along the way. Were I to attempt to name them all, I would surely leave someone out so I'll just say you know who you are.

A big thank you to Mountain View Presbyterian Church for deciding to make The Phoenix Dream Center and the fight against human trafficking one of their missions. It was at a meeting there in 2016 that I decided I needed to use my book to raise awareness in an audience that, like myself, would probably not pick up a book on this modern-day slavery. So thank you readers for helping me achieve my goal.

ABOUT THE AUTHOR

Barbara J. Desman has always been a storyteller; just ask her family and friends. She is now enjoying committing her stories to the page. Her career in the airline industry afforded her the opportunity to explore and observe the culture, people, and sights of many domestic and international destinations.

Barbara has written numerous short stories and her essay, *Why We Didn't Tell*, was published in biostories.com. Her stated intention for this chapter of her life is to become the Grandma Moses of Prose.

Barbara writes from Arizona with her companion Toy Fox Terrier, Bubbles, at her feet.